THIRTEEN DIAMOND LAKE POINT

THIRTEEN DIAMOND LAKE POINT
A SPIRITED MYSTERY

MARY K CRAWFORD-LORFINK

First Printing: October 2023
First Edition

Paperback ISBN: 978-1-955541-27-5
eBook ISBN: 978-1-955541-28-2
Hardcover ISBN: 978-1-955541-29-9
LCCN: 2023917797

Cover Image: ©iStock.com/lenanet
Cover and interior design by Ann Aubitz

Published by FuzionPress
1250 E 115th Street
Burnsville, MN 55337
Fuzionpress.com
612-781-2815

DEDICATION

New Year's Visitation

Years since I left my body,
floating on the shimmering sounds
of a saxophone solo

Years shared in the sultry night air
over a steel-top table
under the starry twinkle
and string of overhead light

Years Manhattan's ineffable spirit
rising spectacular skyline view
from our bedroom window

Years of your reflection
passing in a mirror

Years as fast as dreams allow
Years drifting above our heads,
like clouds

Years of surrounding sky,
the color in your eyes

Years dusky hued and earthbound –
that went spectacularly awry,
twisting fate dispassionately
through my heart

Years the scent of roses in the air,
the kindness of friends,
family kept me alive

Years of story, myth, truth
Years since I left my body,
midair, midlife

Delicious memories of the saxophone
beautiful like the sunset

by   Mary K Crawford-Lorfink

TABLE OF CONTENTS

CHAPTER ONE

HELP WANTED

August 2003

Janet pauses, coffee cup in hand, as she rereads the ad.

Prominent Minnesota-based philanthropist seeking Assistant with strong secretarial and computer skills to assist with personal and business engagements. Confidentiality is a must. Excellent references are required.

Circling the ad in blotchy red ink, Janet takes a final sip from her mug of coffee, then folds the Help Wanted section of the newspaper, stuffing it into an oversized floral tote bag.

She stands stiffly, aware of the tension in her shoulders and neck. The backs of her legs and thighs damp with perspiration, the result of sitting too long with her legs pressed against the rigid vinyl of the café booth. She feels all of her 47 years and takes a moment to allow the blood to flow back into her numb legs before heading out the restaurant door.

The concrete sidewalk outside *Main Street Deli and Café* is wafting up waves of heat and humidity, intermingled with the foul odors of unwashed cement and rotting food from an over-heated metal dumpster. Janet consciously challenges herself to resist the sickening feeling rising from the pit of her stomach into her throat.

A short distance up the street, a small gathering of city workers labor over an open manhole cover. A stinging cloud of loose sand whips up around them and spirals skyward, then airborne, carrying the same gritty excess of dust and gravel toward her. She winces as the loose gray gravel pelts her bare arms and face. The gritty assault clings to her, and she tastes the dry sand sticking to her lips. Then, desperate to escape the oppressive heat and abrasive sting of gravel, she quickens her steps and hurries up the short city block.

"Thank God!" she says, stepping into a refreshing blast of icy circulating air. Her voice bounces through the spacious apartment lobby without notice. The two-story hotel-style lobby has been recently renovated with white marble flooring and a decorative slab of frosted glass mounted with steel pins on a wall of cherry wood. The ambiance, now a trendy vibe of wood, glass, and metal, could be described as upscale smart, but seated behind an imposing block of matching cherry wood desk, the security guard has his head down, sound asleep, impervious to any activity in the lobby.

The elevator doors ding open, and she is again grateful that her studio apartment's hallway and narrow confines are as chilled as the lobby. She dumps her floral tote bag on a cushy chair and removes the newspaper. But before picking up the telephone receiver, she takes a deep, relaxing, yoga-style breath hoping that the recent jolt of caffeine will enhance her energy and focus rather than betray jittery nerves.

A soft-spoken woman answers the phone. "Good afternoon, Ava Fleming office of Philanthropy, Elaine speaking."

The woman's soothing tone causes Janet to smile and relax into the conversation.

"Hello, my name is Janet Kelly, and I'm calling about the ad you placed in *Minneapolis Daily News* for a personal assistant."

Elaine's response is clear and rehearsed, "Please fax us your resume, and we'll get back to you if we are interested. Are you ready for the FAX number?"

As left-over collateral from her New York job, which she occasionally worked from home, Janet had inherited a fax machine now synced to her Minneapolis landline telephone. She promptly faxes her resume to Elaine twice, just to be certain.

Later that evening, Janet receives a phone call from Ava Fleming, President of the Fleming Family Foundation. Ava's diction is precise. Her voice quietly modulated and trained like that of a Shakespearean thespian.

Fleming? Janet wonders. *As in Sebastian Fleming? As in Beverly Rose Fleming?* She recalls two actors from the Golden Age of Hollywood who recently passed, with the Fleming family name. *Is Ava part of that Fleming family?*

Janet then wonders if 'eccentric millionaire, heiress, or diva' might also apply to Ava but decides it would be unkind to assume and withholds judgment. But in her next breath of conversation, Ava's questions to Janet seem more like questions one might ask a new neighbor if you bumped into them at the supermarket.

In an even-toned robotic voice, as if reading from a list of prepared questions, Ava asks:

"Are you married?"

"No."

"Do you live alone?"

"Yes."

"Do you have pets?"

"No."

"Do you have children?"

"No."

"Do you have family in the area?"

"Yes."

"Do you have a boyfriend?"

"No."

Janet draws a long, patient breath and slows her speech, determined to answer Ava's questions more conversationally, with thoroughly thought-out complete sentences.

"My full name is Janet Faith Kelly. I'm originally from Minneapolis, Minnesota. Seventeen years ago, I married a man from the East Coast and moved to his home state of New Jersey. My husband, John, and I commuted daily from Jersey City to New York City. John worked in lower Manhattan, the financial district, and I worked uptown near Rockefeller Plaza for a business magazine."

Janet fidgets with a comfort-grip ballpoint pen, twirling it like a miniature baton between her fingers, then pacing as far as the tangled telephone cord will allow.

"I was the Reprint Sales Manager for a publication

called *SUCCESSFUL*. My job was to contact entrepreneurs featured in our bi-monthly magazine and offer them custom-designed, copyrighted reprints of articles they were featured in."

Janet stops pacing and glances down at the two-page resume spread across her desk. Again, she wants to be precise. "I helped create reprints by working with the featured entrepreneur and a graphic designer. The client then used the reprints as marketing material."

Ava says nothing. Janet continues. "Their stories amazed me. How each entrepreneur overcame setbacks and discouragement through focus and commitment was inspirational. By far, the most interesting job I've ever had."

Still, with no comment from Ava, Janet adds, "Before that, I worked as a legal secretary for an insurance company near Rockefeller Plaza."

"How did you meet your husband?" Ava asks.

"Uh...sure," Janet answers hesitantly. She looks past her patio windows onto her partially shaded cement balcony, where an outdoor planter overflows with red geraniums. "He was on a business trip, and I was working at a jewelry kiosk when he stopped to purchase a gold-plated '*leaf*' necklace. *Nature's Jewels* was the name of the company. They dipped leaves and acorns in gold, then sold them on a gold-plated chain as a necklace. A little side job I worked in downtown Minneapolis," Janet answers.

"Who did he buy the jewelry for?"

"Uh...He told me the necklace was for his mother."

"Was it?"

"It was. That's the kind of guy he was."

"Why did you move back to Minneapolis?"

"My husband died, and I wanted to be near family. I still consider Minneapolis *home*. *It's* where I grew up. I live in downtown Minneapolis, just a few blocks from my parent's apartment. For the past two years, I've been working secretarial temp jobs. I took some time off after my husband passed to relocate back to Minneapolis."

Janet remembers reading somewhere that *all lives end the same way. Between the start and the finish, it's the stories that count.* Clearly, Ava appreciates an exciting story. Either way, Janet finds herself easily engaged in conversation with Ava. It comes naturally, and Ava's interest in Janet's private life, though mostly inappropriate, is somewhat touching.

When Ava asks Janet about her additional work history, Ava is quiet, waiting perhaps for a twist in the 'employment' plot or for Janet to describe a despicable past employer. Ava wants to hear another 'story'.

Janet has a slew of work stories dating back thirty years, beginning with her first job as a car hop at the neighborhood A&W Root Beer stand. At this moment, however, hovering above the small wooden desk in the frigid air of her downtown Minneapolis apartment, the past feels irrelevant, small, and unimpressive. The only part of her story worth mentioning are the years shared with her late husband and one favorite job, working for a New York magazine.

What's the point? Flits through her mind. *My husband is gone, and my favorite job is now in the past.*

"Why don't you use your married name?" her husband had asked one weekday evening.

"What?" Janet responded, caught off-guard and not fully understanding the question.

"The inside title page of *Successful* magazine," he answered, holding the open magazine with both hands and wondering eyes. "It says Janet Kelly, Reprint Sales Manager."

Janet could hear the hurt in his voice. He'd been stuck with the last name 'Gottschald' his entire life. The name was all right if you could pronounce it correctly, but ***Janet Kelly-Gottschald*** wasn't exactly poetic. She preferred her maiden name, Janet Kelly.

"Space is limited, and they won't let me hyphenate my last name." she lied.

She reimagines the moment. This time, she is honest and sympathetic. The kind of partner she should have been years ago. Had she known then that her husband was ill, was, in fact, dying from exposure to the defoliant Agent Orange used during the Vietnam War and his days serving as a Marine, she would have gently held his hand in hers and replied, "I'll put in a request to change my printed name to Janet Gottschald on Monday. The important thing is that you are here, and you're with me now."

Then with a mix of hopelessness and nostalgia, Janet blurts out, "Did you ever see the Christmas tree at Rockefeller Center, sparkling and beautiful, or the angels of light with trumpets lining Rockefeller Plaza?"

Janet's eyes tear up. "I loved Christmas in New York! The window displays at Lord and Taylor! Have you ever seen the Rockettes dance as toy soldiers at Radio City Music Hall?"

Ava's voice rises with sudden interest. "Yes!" she replies, "I was with my mother and father at Radio City Music Hall for several movie premiers and award ceremonies. I always sat between them!"

This memory rings a clear note of joy for Ava.

It then occurs to Janet that the few jobs she left or was let go from didn't hold her interest. Temp jobs (too temporary); Legal Secretary (working for a dark-eyed woman with a British accent who refused to make eye contact and spoke to Janet with contempt); Loan Officer (monotonous and too much paperwork); Waitress (dead-end). She needed freedom and space to approach her problems creatively. There was nothing to be ashamed of, all her paychecks were hard-earned, but she craved variety and independence. Her favorite job, working for the business magazine, *Successful,* constantly challenged her imagination and literary skills. The magazine's business was conducted in a cluttered environment of cardboard boxes piled high and packed full of magazine back issues. She sat in a semicircle of co-workers, each absorbed in their inspired musings, scribbling ideas into spiral notebooks, seated on folding chairs, waiting to discuss upcoming issues as the office cat looked on. The job was perfect. The more demanding and eccentric the job was, the more it seemed to interest and motivate her.

Working for Ava Fleming might hold her interest with the key elements of a great adventure or, at the very least, a welcome diversion from the dismal slump of recent events in her life. It intrigued her. And, yes, she was interested.

The following day, Janet receives a phone call from Elaine inviting her for a private interview at Ava Fleming's home office, located along the scenic shores of Diamond Lake.

"Excellent!" Janet says and immediately calls her mother, "Mom! I'm heading out for a job interview tomorrow at the private home of Ava Fleming on Diamond Lake!"

Janet's mother is startled by her daughter's uncharacteristic burst of enthusiasm. Then with an underlying tone of concern, she lowers her voice, "You're driving to Diamond Lake for a job interview? Isn't that a bit far from downtown?"

"Mom, you're missing the point. I have a job interview with *Ava Fleming* tomorrow morning. Do you recall the Flemings of Hollywood? The actor and actress?"

"Hmmm, yes," her mother answers slowly.

"Do you mean Fleming as in *Sebastian Fleming* and *Beverly Rose Fleming*? I adored Beverly Rose Fleming in that romantic comedy; what was it called? I can't remember, anyway, I adored her! I think she's passed. There was another Fleming, a daughter, I believe. What happened to her?"

"Mom! That's who I'm talking about. I believe *Ava Fleming* is their daughter! Apparently, she is now President of the *Fleming Family Foundation*. Her parents have passed on, and now she's a philanthropist needing a personal assistant."

"She's *a what*?"

"A philanthropist. She donates her time and money to charitable organizations."

"What do you know about philanthropy?"

"Nothing, but I can learn!"

"That's quite a long drive to Diamond Lake," her mother repeats.

"They gave me driving directions. But listen, I really want this job. I'm not interested in working another secretarial 'temp' job. So, say a prayer for me, will you?"

Reviewing her resume later that evening, Janet memorizes the impressive points of her work history. She files it away in the business attaché she brought from New York City, hoping it will add a sparkle of success to the job interview. She then hangs a conservative gray business jacket and lightweight pair of pressed slacks over her desk chair and pulls a soft, sleeveless white blouse from her closet that will be perfect without the jacket if the office is as steamy inside as it is outside. Janet believes the job is a long shot. Most likely, a dozen other applicants have applied for this high-profile position. Still, she feels jazzed by the tantalizing prospects of the unconventional ad and the opportunity to drive far, far away from the downtown noise and air pollution. That in itself is enough for Janet to feel happy about.

Chapter Two
The Hollywood Heiress

The next morning, heading west on an open four-lane stretch of highway, Janet feels conflicted about the opportunity before her.

Diamond Lake was well-known for its excessive wealth and spectacular lakeshore estates. Still, it had been several months since she had ventured outside her downtown neighborhood and close ring of suburbs, and it left her with a mixed air of uncertainty as to whether she would be able to follow the directions Elaine provided.

Will she be able to navigate the private, secluded roads around Diamond Lake? Will she blend into this wealthy, established community?

Downtown, with its fast-paced, nerve-racking wail of sirens, its pounding reverberation of ongoing construction, and low groaning back-up beeps of dump trucks, is chaotic like New York City. Janet had grown accustomed to the halting motion of downtown traffic, interspersed with the daredevil dart of pedestrians.

As excited as she had been about this job prospect the day before, she now feels less certain of her ability to understand the privileged lifestyle of a Hollywood heiress, of visiting the stylish home of a well-known socialite.

Janet drives toward the boundless expanse of stark blue horizon. Adjusting her rearview mirror, she looks back at the hazy downtown Minneapolis skyline, smoldering under a smoggy brown cloud that hovers like a lost soul floating in purgatory. The city is in a state of fatigue due to the overuse of electrical circuits, power surges, and seemingly endless brick, concrete, and steel structures, blocking any hope of a passing breeze.

It then surprises Janet to realize that the further away from the city she drives, the happier she begins to feel as the peripheral scenery whizzing by gradually transforms into a carpet of greenery. There is little to obstruct her view of the wide-open suburban landscape, with the exception of a raised American Flag snapping in the wind above a GM car dealership, a rectangular six-story apartment complex, and one building still under construction with streams of daylight poking through in a myriad of angles.

Then, passing a distant grove of trees, she sees the glittering reflection of a small pond. Checking her odometer, she is now twenty-one miles outside of downtown Minneapolis and turning onto a curving two-lane road that follows the winding shoreline of Diamond Lake. A jagged-edged wooden street sign indicates she is driving along Blue Heron Drive. After another mile or two, she turns right onto Ladyslipper Lane, and her car bumps up onto a shaded, narrowing road reinforced with heavy fresh layers of velvety black asphalt. She tunnels through a quiet spread of ancient cottonwoods, the mighty tree trunks dividing into thick branches and shading the road ahead with their leafy canopy of dark foliage.

Janet slows down, afraid she might miss an upcoming turn and cautiously cruises through a private community of homes hidden behind brick walls. Tendrils of white and blue morning glories attached to the red brick walls are offset by rambling rose bushes and one man-sized Grecian lawn statue of a virile winged Cupid, poised with bow and arrow, knee-deep in tufted, native prairie grass. The weathered statue with its streaked greenish-brown complexion appears to have been forgotten, and it's impossible to determine which sequestered home this naked messenger of love might belong to.

At the row of white mailboxes, Janet turns right again as instructed by Elaine. She continues on a steep downhill descent that rolls her forward like a guest at a Hollywood awards ceremony, being received upon the official *Red Carpet*. She is driving out onto a stretch of property that feels removed from the rest of the world by a long draw of peninsula, and the private drive changes from heavy asphalt to Victorian-pink pavers. Several splendid acres of manicured lawn spread out, with ornamental hedges and well-spaced circular groupings of mature evergreen, maple, and cottonwood trees. It feels as though she has entered a movie star's secluded waterfront property.

Driving toward her destination, the private drive slowly rises, at once revealing a sprawling cream-colored brick mansion with a steep slant of dark purplish gray roof. The roof reaches skyward in full sunlight over the front entrance: a vaulted double-height projection of slate grey suspended between two densely layered stone-on-stone columns, and although the home is remarkable in size, it flows naturally with the landscape.

Janet sees a designated parking area off to the far right and parks her car under the cantilevered eaves of a three-car garage. She exits her vehicle with a slow, disbelieving look of amazement.

She is in stun mode. The fresh lake air is the purest and most refreshing she has ever inhaled. She can hear the rhythmic sounds of lapping water hidden behind an even row of arborvitaes. Carefully, she brushes between the tall shrubs and finds herself standing on a grassy three-foot embankment overlooking the crystal blue sparkles of Diamond Lake. Thirty feet out, a wooden weather-worn recreational swimming dock bobs in sync with the motion of the lake. Squinting into the sunlight, she sees an island off in the distance but cannot see beyond it.

She imagines Diamond Lake 10,000 years ago as a glacial ice sheet. She envisions the immense glacier retreating and the hollowed space filling with glacial melt as fresh and cold and deep blue as it appears at this very moment. *This is a lake, untouched by time,* she murmurs.

Janet turns back and follows the pink stone walkway to the home's front entrance. She rings the doorbell. Singing bells can be heard echoing throughout the house, and an attractive blonde woman in her late thirties answers the door with an apricot poodle hugging her ankles.

"Hi, you must be Janet?" she says cheerfully. "We're expecting you! I'm Fiona, and this is Minka, who apparently can't wait to meet you!" she laughs. The miniature poodle hovers near Fiona's feet, tail wagging.

"Please come in. Would you care for a glass of iced tea?"

A white tea towel is draped casually over Fiona's shoulder. She is comfortably dressed in a loose blouse and slacks, and Janet assumes she is the housekeeper. She brings Janet a tall glass of tea with clinking ice cubes and a floating slice of lemon, then escorts her to the lower level of the home. The carpeted stairway to the lower level has a plush, expensive bounce, and the house has the overly fresh scent of professional cleaning products. She glances to the left and sees what appears to be the theater room with several rows of red leather recliners facing an enormous screen.

At the far end of the room, a matching set of traditional fabric swivel chairs are dwarfed by a wooden, seven-foot-tall giraffe. The giraffe's dappled, emerald-hued neck tapers upward to its narrow, hand-painted face, and its frozen expression asks, *"Where am I?"*

The room has a hushed, abandoned feel. The furniture, cushions, and carpet hold no impression of life or use.

Fiona leads Janet to the threshold of a two-person office, then heads back upstairs. A blue-eyed woman in her mid-sixties glances up from her desk. Her lustrous white hair and pale pinkish skin give her a swan-like appearance, with a long dancer's neck and smooth purposeful pose.

"Hello. Welcome. I'm Elaine, I do the bookkeeping, and this is Mindy, our Foundation Accountant."

Elaine stands and welcomes Janet with a gentle handshake. "Mindy and I will be interviewing you this afternoon."

Smiling broadly, Mindy stands to shake Janet's hand firmly. She is dressed in a squarely cut beige cotton jacket and matching pants that give her a sporty athletic appearance. Janet nods "hello" and smiles. "What a beautiful home office you have here!"

Janet looks around the room, thinking it feels more like a model office showroom on a commercial brochure than a hard-working financial office. She feels Elaine and Mindy's curious stare and responds by handing each woman a copy of her resume. The resume is a welcome diversion from the pressure of the moment.

"So, Janet," Elaine says, "tell us a bit about yourself and what interested you about the position?"

Then, with a warm surge of confidence, Janet begins reading from her resume, explaining her work history, bullet point by bullet point, as Elaine and Mindy listen, nodding their approval.

"Your job, as Personal Assistant, would be to accompany Ms. Fleming to hosted events," Elaine explains, "keeping track of her calendar and assisting with daily appointments. On occasion, you will be her driver. You will be driving Ms. Fleming in the silver-gray Mercedes you may have noticed parked in the garage. Ms. Fleming is married, and her husband travels. Occasionally she will accompany her husband, and you would be responsible for making *her* travel arrangements. Ms. Fleming's husband has a secretary who handles his travel arrangements."

The three women pause, looking up expectantly as a petite golden-haired woman pokes her head around the corner of the open office doorway, and then slowly emerges into full view. Although it is late morning into early afternoon, the woman is barefoot and dressed in silky layers of a peach-colored nightgown and ankle-length robe. The shimmery ensemble is loosely secured with two oversized floppy ribbons of satin, tied in one loopy bow beneath her chin, spilling over onto her chest. The excessive fabric emphasizes her tiny physique.

The woman's bouncy blonde bob is artfully styled with a wisp of bang, and although Janet assumes the woman to be in her late 60s or early 70s, her skin is smooth and lifted. The woman seems reluctant to step forward and remains framed in the doorway.

Janet takes a step forward and offers to make the introduction. "Hello, I'm Janet Kelly."

Hesitantly, the woman moves toward Janet, offering her pale, placid hand. "Hello, I'm Ava Fleming."

Janet is surprised by Ava's small stature. She had imagined a statuesque, lithe, leading lady, but the woman standing before her appears fragile, delicate, and at most five feet tall. Ava has an ethereal presence, enhanced with a hint of childlike innocence. Her enormous green eyes focus briefly on Janet, then wander off in a far-away gaze. As quickly as Ava has entered the room, she turns away and heads out the door as if someone had called her name; her bare feet leaving sunken impressions in the deep fibers of champagne-colored carpet.

Elaine and Mindy look at each other in agreement, nodding. "This position must be filled as soon as possible," Elaine tells Janet.

"You will be hearing from us," Mindy adds.

"Thank you for this opportunity," Janet responds, somewhat amazed by the simplicity of the interview. It all seemed so effortless.

Following the interview, Janet returns to the outdoor parking area near her car, slipping between the tall green shrub trees to listen again to the lapping waves before her long drive back to Minneapolis.

Looking forward is so much easier than moving forward; she sighs, *but this...I could get used to.*

A shift in the wind blows a heady row of seagrass forward, and she watches it slump over the edge of the embankment. Janet looks beyond the shallow shoreline, where waves crest over smooth moss-covered rocks. A generous wind rushes in, rounding out the sail of a far distant boat and chopping the water with white caps.

Janet feels the seasons of her life in motion with the deep blue lake. Then, a faint breath of wind blows softly over her, drawing her attention, beckoning her into this oasis of abundance and privilege, where house and lake symbiotically co-exist, and the organic beauty of nature is drinkable and intoxicating. A familiar tingling sensation runs over her flesh. She recognizes it as a sign that she is being guided.

The long days of summer are drifting away. She anticipates the withered leaves, the honeyed gold, and crimson blush of autumn. She will lean into this new season of her life. She will surrender to the whispers of her heart and step out in faith.

At once, she is enveloped in an aura of calm. Then, with the gentleness of falling snow, wispy white puffs fill the air. They are tufts of cotton falling from the century-old cottonwood trees populating Ava Fleming's estate. A single, windswept tuft of seeded cotton floats toward her, and she reaches out, watching as it comes to rest upon her open palm. Holding it tenderly, she makes a wish for destiny to take her in a new direction. Then, blowing it away, the cottony fluff carries her wish high, high above Ava Fleming's pale gold-brick mansion and into the powdery blue swirl of the late afternoon sky.

CHAPTER THREE

A LATE-SUMMER SOIREE

J anet eases her eighteen-year-old Honda Accord between two behemoth *SUVs*, hoping to camouflage the fresh dent she noticed last week, returning to her vehicle, bearing a bag of groceries in one arm.

At least have the courtesy to leave a note! She had muttered to herself.

The old Honda had proven to be a reliable source of transportation, and with frequent car washes, she thought it attractive enough. But the recent damage took her geriatric vehicle to another level of *timeworn*, and now there is this eyesore that she has neither the patience nor inclination to repair. Today is another day, however. It is, in fact, her *first day* embarking on a new career in Ava Fleming's sprawling brick mansion.

Janet bows her head and closes her eyes, resting her hands on the steering wheel.

Dear God, Wherever this leads, I know you, and I will write this story together...

Shifting in the driver's seat, Janet opens her eyes. She casts a nervous glance in the rear-view mirror to be sure she's still alone in the outdoor parking area, hoping no one interprets her posture of head bowed with hands resting on the steering wheel as a sign of distress; she quickly searches for something meaningful to pray. The air in the car hangs still as she contemplates her unfinished meditation. Once again, she solemnly bows her head. Then in a flash of inspiration continues...

*Please, God, make this story **interesting**! Thank you, and Amen.*

Satisfied, she smiles, grabs her leather crossbody bag with tassels, and lifts the still-steaming cup of *Caribou* coffee from the console cup holder. She steps through the garage door entrance, dressed conservatively in a lightweight jacket, dress slacks, and dusty-blue polyester blouse.

The silvery luster of Ava's Mercedes Benz washes over her, bringing a wave of uncertainty. *Had she dressed appropriately for her first day? Should she have accessorized with jewelry or a scarf, like the Delta flight attendants she observed flying from New York to Minneapolis?*

What would she wear tomorrow?

Janet never focused on trends or style and bought clothing primarily out of necessity. She fit perfectly into a size twelve outfit at five-foot-seven or five-foot-eight (in a stacked heel), simplifying her shopping experience.

Janet reflects on her working years in Manhattan, where fashion was highly regarded, and clothing options were overwhelming. The previous year's designer trends were always available at a discount. Dresses, pants, and blouses hung in a jumble on rolling racks near the back of the store. She would reach high and tug on a hanger, releasing an item of clothing, thinking, *"Great! I got a deal!* But there was a reason last year's clothing was discounted and assigned to the back wall. The outfit was always less appealing once she brought it home. Discounted and mostly non-returnable, her purchases were often a mistake. No matter, in those days, Janet covered up her clothing with an oversized raincoat or winter coat, depending on the season. She rode the New York subways. *No point in attracting unwanted attention,* she reasoned.

"Why don't you wear fashionable knee-length boots with that outfit?" Her husband had asked one evening as they headed out for dinner.

"Because I don't own any?!?" she answered, waving her arms in the air, exasperated. She expected some form of gratitude for her frugality.

In the financial district of lower Manhattan, her husband, John, was surrounded by men and women who dressed to impress, who wore the couture-grade tailoring of New York City's business and executive class. Not quite to that standard, her husband routinely dressed in suits purchased at a menswear chain offering brand-name attire. They would leave the house together in the morning; she bundled in a raincoat with oversized shoulder pads and sneakers, her husband looking dapper in a classic pinstripe suit and navy necktie.

He looks handsome and business formal, she thought. She never considered what he thought of her fashion choices. She was in her comfort zone and felt loved. That was really all that mattered.

She was no longer in New York City, however. There were different guidelines for dressing in the Midwest. People were outdoorsy and often stepped out in recreational gear without taking a second look in the mirror. Maybe she was overthinking it. The outfit she wore a week ago during the interview was professional enough to land her the job. In addition, Ava had countered her salary request with a higher salary!

"That's not enough money," Ava told Janet over the phone while discussing Janet's salary. Ava then countered with an increase of ten thousand dollars!

Perhaps Ava wanted Janet to dress for success? *To up her game?* Or had Janet's salary request simply been too low? Whatever the reason, on some level, her appearance didn't interfere with her getting the job, and she got a better salary than anticipated, so it was a *Win-win!*

Now with more confidence, Janet passes through the garage and steps into the house via the kitchen entrance, surprising two housekeepers sipping coffee at a circular oak breakfast table.

"Hi! Um, excuse me, ladies. I'm Janet Kelly, Ava Fleming's new assistant."

The women pause to look up but say nothing.

"I believe I saw you both bustling about the day of my interview. It was Fiona who answered the door, however."

"I'm Sarah. This is Bonnie."

"So, Ava has three of you helping her?"

"Yes, Bonnie and I typically work the morning housekeeping shifts. Fiona is here to prepare lunch and dinner."

Sarah, a stout countrified woman, stands slowly, then walks toward the kitchen sink with her coffee cup. "Your first day? I'm sure they're expecting you downstairs. Help yourself to the coffee." She motions to the coffee maker on the counter, "...and *GOOD LUCK* on your first day with Ava!"

Sarah turns to Bonnie, and Janet sees Sarah roll her eyes.

"Oh, thanks, I brought my own," Janet says, drawing back and holding high her paper cup with the leaping *Caribou* coffee logo.

Returning to her place at the table, Sarah shows Bonnie a five-by-seven-inch photograph of a pillowy layer cake shaped like a Bible.

"This is the cake I baked for my granddaughter's confirmation."

Bonnie looks uncertain. "A chocolate Bible? How did you get the edges to look like pages? Good job!"

Bonnie moves in for a closer look, "there's no *'e'* in confirmation!"

Janet, suddenly embarrassed for Sarah, heads quickly downstairs, passing Mindy and Elaine's office on the way to her new office. She sees Elaine on the phone, her platinum hair partially covering the phone receiver. She sees only the back of Mindy's head, then notices the *Outdoor Enthusiast* clothing website spread wide across Mindy's monitor screen.

Janet enters her new office at the end of the hallway and is pleased to see how meticulously clean it appears. Two L-shaped cherry wood executive desks fill the space, with ample room between them. Vertical cherry wood filing cabinets line two of the walls. Displayed on top of the filing cabinets are an assortment of silver-framed photos. One photo shows a woman dressed in a silky, chiffon, V-neck gown with sparkling stones banding the waist. Another photo shows a gentleman dressed in a black and white tuxedo, holding a statuette.

Were these Ava's famous parents? Janet wonders.

The desk phone rings just as she is reaching for a silver framed photo. She moves quickly, fumbling for the receiver as she sets her black tasseled bag on the desk beside her.

"Hello? I mean...Ava Fleming's office."

"Please see me," says the weary voice on the other end, and the phone clicks off.

Perplexed, Janet heads up the stairs thinking she might encounter Ava somewhere along the way...*in a hallway, hopefully...*

Pausing on the upper landing, she hears the faint chatter of housekeepers still in the kitchen, then decides to explore in the opposite direction. She finds her way to the foyer, then down a seemingly endless hallway, passing enormous panes of watery blue stained-glass windows. Her footsteps are surprisingly soft upon the marble flooring. But as she walks, she senses a haunting, solitary presence. She stops, momentarily looking back to see if she is being followed. Powdery sunlight clouds the hallway with silence. It is an atmosphere of both rest and unrest. A shiver runs down her spine as she quickens her pace.

Stopping at the first open doorway, she peers in. The room is dark but lavish, with high-vaulted ceilings and an entire wall of heavy theater-like curtains, most likely covering a span of lakeside windows. Centered against a far wall is the room's showpiece, a ginormous bed anchored to an arching headboard of shimmery fabric, and beneath a puff of peach-colored bedding is the outline of a small body. Only a slender lock of golden hair is visible to Janet from the doorway.

"Oh, hello," Ava's back is to Janet, and her voice is muffled. "I'm not feeling well today. Would you please bring my work up to me?"

"Any work in particular that you might want to address?" Janet asks gently, hoping for clarification.

"My mail," Ava mumbles.

Janet politely obliges, retracing her steps through the eerie stretch of hallway and front foyer. She heads back downstairs, hoping desperately to find a shred of mail to present to Ava. To her relief, an open invitation has been placed in the middle of the smaller two desks by Elaine-she guesses. She picks up the invitation and reads...

Gerald Scott and Sheila Livingston-Scott
invite you to dance the night away, and
Enjoy the beauty of a late-summer sunset.
Our home, Briarcliffe Manor, Diamond Lake
Cocktails and hors d'oeuvres
Friday, September 12th at seven o'clock
RSVP to Rebekah McCall at R.McCall@nsm.com

Janet takes the stairs two at a time with the invitation in one hand and a pad and pen in the other. She follows the quiet hallway back to Ava Fleming's bedroom and knocks softly on the open door.

"I have an invitation for you."

"Ohh-hh-hh Janet," Ava moans. "I'm just not doing well today."

It occurs to Janet that she might rally Ava's spirits by acting as a cheerleader, coaxing her employer into a sunny disposition by reading the aesthetically pleasing invitation with the fancy cursive lettering.

Drawing a deep breath, she composes herself, then reads the card with exaggerated animation as if she were cheering up a sickly child.

After a long moment of silence, Ava mumbles, "Maybe you should go in my place."

Janet holds the textured linen card motionless in her hands. "Well, I don't know anyone," she says, wondering if Ava is serious.

The idea seems a small victory for Ava, and her voice rises, "The party is a few weeks away. You could go with Maxwell!" She props herself up on the pillows with her elbows. "He isn't dating anyone right now and is friends with Sheila."

"Sheila? Maxwell?" Janet manages to say, her voice sounding high-pitched and confused.

"You did say you were single..." Ava sinks back into her mound of pillows. "Maxwell's girlfriend passed in a car accident..."

Janet pauses, considering this information. "I'm so sorry. Was it recent?"

"Three years ago." Ava pulls the silken duvet close to her chest. "The car she was riding in was broadsided." Ava rolls to the left, and her mound of feather bed pillows lets out a whoosh. She closes her eyes.

Janet wonders if this is just Ava thinking out loud. *She did just wake up; maybe she's still half-dreaming?*

She then raises her head slightly and opens her eyes again, "Maxwell was once a professional golfer, you know. His first marriage was to Lucy Bentley, the movie star. I'm friends with Maxwell's mother, Phyllis."

Janet nods, feeling a tightening sensation in her stomach. *Three weeks away?* She would have time to prepare a reasonable excuse. *She doesn't have to go to the party.*

"How would you like me to respond to the invitation?" Janet asks.

"Say 'yes'! You will go, of course!"

Janet stares at the invitation, feeling her heart race, uncertain how she will respond to Ava's party invite-slash-blind date, and wondering what outfit she might be able to pull from her closet.

She leaves Ava's room with the invitation still in hand.

Here I am yet again with another delightful dilemma, she murmurs in a dramatic self-pitying voice. *And I need a surprise blind date like I need an older car with more dents in it!*

Why me? she asks the empty hallway, shaking her head. An overwhelming sense of confusion and self-doubt sweeps through her.

On the other hand... she did have a clingy crushed black velvet dress she bought off a discount designer rack in New York City. She had also learned a thing or two since wearing that dress one other time, which was to choose her undergarments wisely. A visible panty line was a party no-no. Not the impression she cared to leave with the respectable guests of Gerald Scott and Sheila Livingston-Scott's party. This time, she would have a seamless silhouette with a scarf or faux pearls to complete her outfit.

Maybe. She would give it some thought. Even consider the possibility that she might actually *enjoy* herself. There was the slightest chance that she would go on the blind date and to the party with Maxwell - after all.

CHAPTER FOUR
MAXWELL, THE THIRD

D uring her first week as Ava Fleming's Assistant, Janet feels a heightened sense of energy that leaves her in a constant state of preparedness. Elaine pops in with the daily mail, and Janet catches sight of the housekeepers dusting or vacuuming the farthest corners of a spacious room but rarely sees or hears from Ava.

Janet decides to concentrate her efforts on the cherry wood file cabinets lining the walls, noting the various organizations associated with the Fleming Family Foundation. The drawers open to a shaky and sparse arrangement of tabbed, hanging file folders. Within each file folder is a thin paper trail of newsletters and inter-office memos from the various organizations supported by the foundation.

The Vanska Museum of Modern Art, Westminster Symphony Orchestra, the Tyrone Guthrie Theater, North

Star Hospital, and the Diamond Lake Garden Club.

Janet finds a slip of paper announcing a new symphony conductor or communications director or an upcoming gala event, dated three months or sometimes three years earlier. The information ends abruptly, seemingly mid-sentence, and although she's still unclear exactly what role Ava's philanthropy plays within each organization, she perseveres, hoping to educate herself on the inner workings of philanthropy.

Janet quickly concludes that the files are useless and resolves to take copious notes and improve the cataloging of new information.

Occasionally, Ava makes her way downstairs to the office and settles in behind the large L-shaped desk adjacent to Janet's desk. When the office phone rings, Janet answers, "Ava Fleming office of philanthropy."

Most often, callers want a word with Ava. Janet overhears the conversations and realizes that callers are interested in Ava's friendship, money, or both.

"You just want my money," Ava snaps at a caller one morning.

The volume is turned up, and Janet overhears the caller's response, "Yes, we tried asking poor people for money but didn't have much luck."

Ava smiles weakly as Janet stifles a giggle.

♦ ♦ ♦

During her second week, Janet is instructed to drive her employer to Diamond Lake Spa and hair salon appointments in the gleaming silver Mercedes. The outings include impromptu shopping excursions to lakefront upscale boutiques.

Though strikingly old-fashioned, the pastel-colored shops, many with striped awnings, look prosperous. They pass two bookshops with crowded outdoor café bistro tables, a florist, a young mother's store with a good-natured pelican logo fixed to the signage, and a string of quaint dress shops. Each shop is another hidden gem, well-known to locals and the occasional tourist.

Shop owners greet Ava at the door, walking quickly toward her, alert, with shoulders back. Then standing close, as if longtime acquaintances, the proprietor gently touches Ava's arm or hand, leading her to a product display while speaking in steady, low-pitched tones, sharing a bit of gossip and definitely trying to close a sale. When Ava disappears from Janet's sight, the shop owner graciously points in the direction her employer has wandered. Ava takes tiny steps in her size four high-heeled shoes, making it easy for Janet to catch up.

The leisurely outings give Janet a chance to browse a highbrow selection of handmade and vintage items, as well as delight in breathtaking views from the other side of Diamond Lake. Janet squints hard but is unable to see Ava's peninsula.

When she finally drives Ava home, Janet feels as though she is playing the role of 'Chauffeur' in a mid-twentieth-century English drama. She holds the door for her employer and even offers assistance with the seat belt. As she shifts the car into *DRIVE,* she feels the unwavering power and weight of the Mercedes floating down the road, impervious to uneven lakeside terrain. But what she enjoys most is the private, luxurious feel of the interior. Once the doors close, a sound-deadening effect and filtered airflow give the interior a balanced, spa-like quality. The cushioned grip of the leather steering wheel and the polished wood trim throughout the interior introduce her to a comfort she never imagined she would experience. Then in a barely audible voice, she hears herself sigh, *"Ahh..."*

♦ ♦ ♦

"Maxwell's here," Ava announces over the phone intercom mid-morning on Wednesday. It's week three of her new job, and Janet has learned to respond promptly to her employer's announcements, no matter how vague or undefined the task might be.

Janet heads upstairs to meet the elusive Maxwell with an impatient huff. She had not yet fabricated a reasonable excuse to remove herself from the date with him on Friday and now, at the last moment, searches madly for an imaginative way to extend her regrets. Janet has nothing in common with the former athlete and ex-husband of well-known film actress Lucy Bentley. But...*On the other hand*, she has nothing planned for Friday. *It might be okay...* She is a bit curious.

Janet enters the room just as Ava is tearing out a check from her checkbook. Maxwell leans in as Ava hands him the check. The two are seated conversationally on the wide wale orange corduroy furniture in the lounging area, just off the kitchen. Ava sits in a low barrel swivel chair, and Maxwell on the expansive sofa. Daylight from the floor-to-ceiling windows floods the room, washing out Maxwell's pale skin and his tousled *Hugh Grant* light brown hair.

Maxwell has Nordic looks. A tall frame and slender,

narrow features, but his posture is not that of a confident man. His shoulders slump, making him appear time-worn, reminding her of her old Honda Accord. He is less athletic than she had imagined. His long legs look gangly thin, splayed behind the rectangular coffee table positioned too close for his comfort. His dress slacks and sporty designer shirt are pressed and clean, but they overpower him. It's as if he used all his energy getting dressed. As if the effort of simply showing up had exhausted him.

"Janet," Ava says, smiling and looking up, "This is Maxwell Hemingway the third."

"Nice to meet you, Maxwell," Janet says, extending her hand.

Maxwell rises wearily from the couch, standing to shake Janet's hand. He has a gentle grip, and his hand feels smooth and cool.

"Any relation to the writer, Ernest Hemingway?" Janet asks with the nervous flicker of a smile.

"No. Different pronunciation," Maxwell answers flatly. "Nice to meet you, Janet."

Is he joking? Janet wonders. *How many ways are there to pronounce 'Hemingway'?* She glances at Maxwell, but he doesn't seem amused. She then considers that he's been asked this question one too many times and has created a sarcastic response to amuse himself.

Maxwell looks at Janet with disinterest, returning to his seated position on the couch. Maxwell and Ava exchange a look, but she cannot interpret their communication.

"Maxwell will be picking you up after work on Friday to attend Gerald and Sheila's party," Ava says.

"Well...okay," she halfheartedly agrees, looking to

Maxwell for assurance. But Maxwell turns away from Janet to face Ava.

She returns to her lower-level office. An hour later, Ava calls down via the intercom and asks Janet to pop upstairs with the daily mail.

Maxwell and Janet cross paths in the upstairs entrance foyer as he is leaving. He carries an untidy bundle of dress shirts and dangling loose neckties. Maxwell looks down at his feet, purposely avoiding eye contact.

The housekeeper Sarah passes by, noticing Janet's inquisitive look, then whispers, "They're her (Ava's) husband's clothing. Richard won't miss them."

When Janet enters the room, Ava is still seated in the orange barrel chair but now appears with a hot cup of tea that Bonnie has set before her.

"Maxwell is looking forward to your date with him on Friday. Do you know what you will be wearing?" Ava asks.

"A sleeveless crushed black velvet dress with pearls," Janet answers, hoping for her employer's approval.

Ava looks away, disappointed.

What was she expecting? Janet asks herself, feeling somewhat frazzled. *A sequined dress with a pink feather boa?!*

A fashion diva - she most certainly was not!

Then with a quick forced smile, Janet adds, "I meant to ask if it would be okay to leave my car here. I will pick it up after the party."

"Of course. That will be fine."

♦ ♦ ♦

When Maxwell pulls up late Friday afternoon, Janet is

waiting expectantly, seated on the iron garden bench beside Ava Fleming's garage, deep breathing the pure lake air to calm her nerves. She suddenly wishes she had fabricated an alibi to ditch her date with Maxwell, although he doesn't seem threatening or even interested in her.

Still vacillating on her decision to go, she watches warily as his car arcs smoothly to park a short distance from her. He is driving a vintage apple-red Mercedes convertible with the black leather top neatly folded back. Janet stands from her seated position on the garden bench to assess her party escort. His dated convertible reminds her of a friend's dad wishing to recapture the nostalgic moments of his youth.

Maxwell gracefully exits the car, his long legs unfolding from their cramped space below the steering wheel, and Janet wonders why tall men choose to drive small sports cars. Maxwell walks toward Janet with an easy stride. He has an indifferent vibe. Aloof and rehearsed as though he had been introduced to a thousand women before her. His clothes, however, seem carefully chosen. He is dressed in an autumn-toned blazer the color of mulled wine, and a faint pink pinstriped shirt with a navy knit necktie. His skin tone looks bronzed, like he may have applied a self-tanner to his hands and face. She then decides in his favor that he does look healthier with a tan.

Janet imagines a twenty-something, soulful version of Maxwell, of his days as a professional golfer married to the movie star Lucy Bentley. She sees the phantom appearance of a once handsome, confident man.

"You look nice," he says.

"You too," she replies and honestly means it.

She extends her hand, but Maxwell steps forward to lightly embrace her. She holds his embrace for an awkward moment, thinking about *what to do next*. His blazer feels stiff and scratchy against her bare arms. She steps back and circles the car, clumsily fumbling for the low-opening car door.

"And we're off!" Maxwell says as he shifts his sporty red car into gear. They drive up the steep hill, leaving Ava Fleming's mansion like an eye-catching postcard in the distance behind them. They drive several miles along winding *Lady Slipper Lane*, then exit onto yet another darkly shaded street without road signs. Up ahead, a half-dozen uniformed valets are standing by to park cars. Maxwell hops out of his vehicle without comment and leaves Janet to exit alone. A parking valet dashes around the car to assist her.

Looking up, she sees past a low rosy-red brick wall onto a circular drive. Then, slightly aghast, she beholds a baroque manor complete with gargoyles and spires. A dense cover of ground-creeping woody plants has grown vertically, covering the formidable stone walls of the home with clinging variegated ivy. The home has the appearance of Sleeping Beauty's castle before she is awakened with a kiss by Prince Charming.

Janet had mixed feelings, some days quietly looking forward to this curiosity of an event accompanied by a clean-shaven ex-pro athlete with ties to Hollywood luminaries and the delicious assortment of hors d'oeuvres she would be offered along with a carefully selected glass of New Zealand Sauvignon Blanc. But now, all she feels is a flush of adrenaline tingling through her body.

What am I doing here?! I'm way out of my league!

Her New York co-workers told her she resembled the popular American singer-songwriter Melissa Manchester. They all agreed, same wild, bouncy waves of dark hair and deep-set brown eyes, but that was it. It was nice to receive the compliment, but she saw little resemblance between herself and Melissa Manchester. Janet didn't think of herself as showy or glamorous. She was mostly thinking 'resourceful and capable'. Janet was *most comfortable* in buttery soft slip-on leather loafers, a stretch denim jacket embroidered with something whimsical on the pocket, and a well-worn pair of faded jeans. Her unruly shoulder-length hair pulled back in a scrunchie.

For this evening, she had freed her hair from the scrunchie and taken time with a little extra styling gel and a few well-timed turns of a curling iron to tame her cascading waves into a smooth, polished look. She had also followed Elaine's suggestion (which she was planning to wear anyway) of the simple sleeveless crushed black velvet dress and a string of faux pearls with matched earrings, *but was it enough?*

Together, Maxwell and Janet ascend a set of palatial monochromatic steps. Flickering gas-lit sconces frame the doorway, casting a warm yellow glow over two gigantic containers of rounded boxwoods and trailing ivy. Honey-toned cathedral doors stand open, creating an arched entrance, both formal and a touch medieval, with matching black cast iron door knockers. Janet steps inside, pausing in the foyer, taking in the home's interior. It is brightly lit with sparkling chandeliers and a blur of candlelight.

Party guests are scattered throughout a grand ballroom, spilling out onto a garden patio. Folks linger outdoors beside an in-ground pool shooting narrow translucent streams of brilliantly colored water straight into the air, then falling with a splash and gurgle into the pool's center.

This must be how the royals live, she muses.

Guests are playfully dressed. One man in salmon pink pants has a bold fishing lure motif stamped up and down his pant legs and a coordinating salmon-pink golf shirt.

Ralph Lauren? Janet wonders.

He is holding his martini glass at a precarious angle as the olive bobs about like a fishing lure, accessorizing his outfit. He gestures dramatically with his free hand, entertaining a group of amused women dressed in flirty pastel dresses, some with lacey wide-brimmed hats.

Janet and Maxwell pause beside a glossy black concert piano listening as the tuxedoed pianist bobs and leans his way along the keyboard, performing Andrew Lloyd Webber's 'Memory' from the musical 'Cats'. The sound resonates throughout the ballroom. It's a crowd-pleaser, and guests are smiling, enjoying the lively ambiance of the soiree. Janet feels the party's energy lift her to a place somewhere beyond her earthly self.

This is surreal, she whispers. She suddenly feels buoyant as a helium-filled balloon.

As they cross the room, Maxwell excuses himself and then returns with two pale orange glasses of champagne. He hands a fluted champagne glass to Janet.

"To new beginnings," he says, raising his glass.

"Yes, *and to new experiences!*" Janet says with emphasis.

"Where are the host and hostess?" she asks.

"Standing over there, near the piano." Maxwell nods

in their direction. "They have been a couple for as long as I can remember. This party is mostly a gathering of their old and not-so-old friends," he says with a smirk on his thin lips.

Just then, Sheila Livingston-Scott, the hostess, crosses the room in a glittering gold cocktail dress and creamy patent leather high-heels with a relaxed and polished gait.

"Nice to see you, Maxwell. Who's the lovely lady with you?"

"This is Janet, Ava Fleming's new assistant. Unfortunately, Ava wasn't able to make it tonight."

Sheila seems to take Ava's absence in stride. "Give my regards to Ava then, will you dear? Lovely to meet you, Janet."

"What a wonderful way to celebrate the end of summer! Your party is absolutely amazing, and what a fabulous home you have!" she gushes.

Sheila, about to turn, stops, then faces Janet with a generous smile.

"Yes, Briarcliffe Manor has been in the family for generations. It is our ancestral home. My Grandmother held summer cotillion balls during her day in this home. I was introduced to Gerald at one of those affairs, and we've been a couple ever since," she says graciously.

From across the room, Gerald sees his wife talking to Janet and gives her a nod. Sheila acknowledges her husband with a slight wave of her hand, then turns back to Janet. For a crazy moment, Janet imagines Gerald with a black eye patch. Sheila's husband has a James Bond 007 relaxed stance and the confident look of a Bond character. One of the good guys.

As Sheila and Janet continue making each other's

acquaintance, Maxwell becomes distracted by a glamorous middle-aged woman entering the room. She is dazzling in her silk crepe rose-print dress and dark up-sweep of carefully coiffed raven hair. She wears flashy drop diamond earrings and an exquisite wedding ring on her well-manicured left hand. She catches Maxwell's eye and smiles slyly, her crescent moon-shaped mouth a sensuous fiery red.

Soon she is joined by a man Janet assumes to be her husband as he places his arm possessively around her slender waist. Maxwell abruptly sets his empty glass on a passing tray and looks around the room uneasily.

"Please excuse me. I'll be back," he tells Janet.

Janet then watches as the glamorous woman with showy diamonds exits the great room. The woman's husband is left standing near the baby grand piano, holding his crystal glass of amber bourbon, absorbed in conversation with another guest. He appears overdressed for the occasion in a silvery-gray suit with a white carnation tucked into his lapel, perhaps compensating for his aging, small, rounded stature.

Janet has an eerie sense of *déjà vu. Is* it F. Scott Fitzgerald's novel, *The Great Gatsby,* full of seduction and obsession? It's not the year 2003, it's the *Roaring Twenties,* and any minute now, Daisy Fay Buchanan and Jay Gatsby will make their grand entrance.

Meanwhile, here she waits, fresh from her sincere and radiant world, now but a decoy for a socially elite woman and Maxwell's lusty appetites. She anticipated her evening to be punctuated with some surprise but certainly had not imagined Maxwell sneaking off for a clandestine meeting with his lady love.

I wonder if Ava knows of Maxwell's illicit affair, Janet wonders. Then suspects that it's not his first.

It's true. Echoes of *The Great Gatsby* can be overheard in conversation: "Oh, the boat! Yes, it's the envy of Diamond Lake. Custom hand-built by the Amish and Mennonite communities, out of wood...the craftsmanship is classic."

"Will you be visiting your home in Palm Springs this season?"

"Yes, last time we visited, we arrived unannounced only to find our housekeeper had moved in! Caught her *living* in our Palm Springs home!"

"What did you do?"

"After dismissing her, changed the locks, of course!"

"The broiled lobster tails are divine; you must try them!"

Spirits of glitz and glam are haunting this high-society soiree, but Janet is determined to enjoy this once-in-a-lifetime event with or without the party-loving playboy, Maxwell. Easing her way through the crowded room, she helps herself to the veal tartare drizzled with a warm white sauce from a butler-passed tray and another glass of champagne.

The view from the garden terrace is spectacular.

Janet contemplates the evening sky's orangey glow with a surreal calm that fills her with a profound sense of purpose and meaning. The mix of party sounds grows hushed, distant, and forgotten.

She picks a hibiscus flower from a nearby planter and places the red flower behind her ear while remembering that in fairy tales and myths, people are warned not to eat from the strange place they've lost themselves in, or they won't be able to leave it.

As the sun disappears from the horizon, she wonders if this is where she is truly meant to be.

She senses someone standing beside her.

"Hello," he says.

Janet turns to see a six-foot-plus man with a radiant smile, his white teeth flashing in the deepening light. He's dressed effortlessly in a balance between sporty and elevated. He's tie-less, and the top buttons of his white dress shirt are left casually undone.

"Oh, hello!"

"I'm Keegan Scott, your neighbor. Well, Ava Fleming's neighbor, that is. Sheila suggested I introduce myself."

"Nice to meet you, Keegan," Janet says, turning to take in a full-body view.

Keegan has a beaming smile but gives off gentle, laid-back vibes. He impresses her as the outdoorsy type with his athletic build and tousled sun-bleached hair.

"You live where in relation to Ava's home?"

"Oh, just a short distance from Ava in a simple lakeside cottage off *Lady Slipper Lane*. I don't live far from Mariner's Bay, the swimming beach with the floating dock?"

"Sure, I've seen that dock from Ava's shoreline!" Janet is pleased to discover they have this in common. She knows the shoreline around Ava's home! No matter how trivial, she can at least discuss the lake with him.

Keegan motions toward two slatted wooden deck chairs facing the lake. They sit, then turn to look at each other a second time. Janet holds her champagne glass close to her body like a prop, glancing from the lake to Keegan. She feels an instant attraction and is surprised by her intuitive response to this stranger.

"Have you had a chance to tour the Diamond Lake community? Any favorite restaurants yet?"

"I've picked up lunch from that co-op on the corner of Diamond Lake Road," Janet answers. "Also, a big fan of Caribou Coffee."

Keegan leans forward, encouraging Janet with his undivided attention. She is flattered that he seems interested, and the effect of the champagne emboldens her.

"Part of my new job is driving Ava to her various appointments. I've driven her to hair salons, spa appointments, and even retail boutiques. It's rather fun, actually! Turns out I'm more adventurous than I thought, and I love exploring the neighborhood, if you can call it that!"

Keegan smiles. "Yeah, I get it; the houses are next to impossible to spot from the road. So many private estates."

When she mentions how she almost lost her way returning from the opposite side of Diamond Lake, Keegan suggests a shortcut along a quiet side street. "Diamond Lake is roughly 175 miles of shoreline," he says.

"I hope Ava's appointments stay close to the lake. As long as I can see the water, I'll have a point of reference."

"That sounds like a good idea! Just follow the shoreline, and you should be okay. Do you have family living nearby?"

"I do! My parents live just a few blocks from my downtown Minneapolis apartment."

"What do they think of your new job on Diamond Lake?" he asks with a twinkle in his eye.

Janet considers what to say next. Should she tell

Keegan that she has a 'hippie heritage'? That her mother was the first woman she had known to wear Australian Kangaroo-leather hiking boots? That when Janet's mother walked through a restaurant, following a day of hiking through Carver County State Park with her husband, people would stare pointedly at her high-top hiking boots with open disdain? She briefly considers, then answers with a shrug, "My parents would literally freak out if they saw this place! When I was growing up, they spent their vacations hiking through state parks, snacking on honey-baked granola, and carrying a hiking pole with bells attached to frighten off the bears. This is a far cry from that!"

Keegan leans back in his chair and laughs a spontaneous, genteel laugh.

"What about you, Keegan Scott, any relation to our host, Gerald Scott?"

"Yes indeed! Gerald's my uncle!"

"So, you live in a simple lakeside cottage, and your aunt and uncle live in this fairy tale castle?!"

"Yes, but they are *anything but* pretentious!"

Janet nods without confidence, wondering how Sheila Livingston-Scott would react to seeing her mother's combat boots and zip-lock bag of homemade granola. Janet was a teenager in the 70s when it was cool to be anti-establishment. Hiking boots were becoming fashionable. She considers both her mother and father idealists: free-thinking and uninhibited. She wonders whether her parents would approve of this soiree or think it a ridiculous waste of time and money. And yet, to her surprise, Keegan is refreshingly down-to-earth and pleasant. He seems to be an outlier among this group of highbrow party guests. *Was he obligated to attend because Gerald Scott is his uncle?*

The warm Indian Summer breeze blows off the lake, ruffling her hair and sending a chill down her bare arms. As she brushes strands of hair from her face, she turns to see Maxwell approaching. Janet is so smitten with Keegan that she has almost forgotten Maxwell. After what feels like well over an hour, Maxwell reappears, looking morose.

"Ready to go?" he asks flatly.

"Sure," she replies coolly. "Maxwell, you may already know Keegan Scott, one of Ava Fleming's neighbors?"

"Yeah, hi Keegan. Keegan and I go way back. Ready to go, Janet?" Maxwell asks with a stony expression.

"Maybe I'll see you around town?" Keegan asks Janet as he gently adjusts the drooping red flower behind her ear.

"That would be lovely," Janet says, slowly turning to leave.

She can't help but wonder what happened during Maxwell's absence. Based on his irritability, it appears his rendezvous with the glamorous *Liz Taylor* look-alike was a disappointment.

Maxwell drives Janet back to Ava's house in brooding silence and pulls into a parking space near Janet's car. The outdoor light sensors blink on. He leans in for a kiss, and in a moment of weakness and curiosity, Janet kisses him back. But Maxwell wants more. He pulls her close. The gear shift is at an uncomfortable angle, but he manages to slide his hand around her back, then forward, groping her breast. She pulls away, shocked that he would be so presumptuous but also mildly wary that Maxwell is her new employer's family friend. She wonders what the wealthy women see in him. She finds him distant, thoughtless, and a mediocre kisser.

"Should I meet you at your downtown apartment?" he asks without hesitation.

"Ahhh...*NO!*" Janet almost shouts her answer. Then, infuriated by his arrogance, she grabs her purse from the car's floor and reaches for the door handle.

"Come on, what are you waiting for, Janet?! It's not like you're getting any younger!"

Appalled, Janet quickly exits Maxwell's car, slamming the door hard behind her. She somehow manages to say, "Good night," without looking back. Why she even kissed him irritates her. *What was I thinking?* she wonders angrily, wiping his kiss from her mouth with the back of her hand.

She turns toward her car, grateful for Ava's floodlights illuminating the outdoor parking area and curbside shrubbery, then listens as Maxwell's car screeches off into the night. She mentally erases Maxwell from this evening, choosing instead to dwell on the blissful hour spent with Keegan Scott.

Janet drives her dented Honda home in a dreamy state of optimism, believing she will see Keegan again. Turning on the radio to **KOOL 109,** she catches the ***Golden Oldies*** Friday night special. A popular doo-wop group from the late 1950s is crooning the timeless lyrics to a sentimental song that conjures up feelings of nostalgia and romance. Janet's thoughts turn immediately to Keegan. His smile and the memory of his lingering touch fill her with a rush of emotion as she floats somewhere between celestial and earthbound.

Turning up the volume, Janet sings along in her loud alto voice, straining to reach the high notes, her heart swelling at the message of standing alone, then turning to find a love of her own.

Janet feels like a lovestruck adolescent, and to her surprise, a tear rolls down her cheek.

Maybe it's been a long, tiring week, or maybe it's been too long since she felt a twinge of romance.

"How was your evening with Maxwell?" Her mother asks Janet the following day.

"Maxwell is handsome, but he has some serious character defects," she tells her mother. Janet recalls Maxwell's narcissistic behavior. His blatant disregard for her was eye-opening and a huge turn-off. "The party and guests were another story; however, both lovely and enjoyable!"

Janet smiles, recalling Keegan's relaxed mannerisms, friendly blue eyes, and welcoming warmth – and for the next few moments, she feels lifted again, above the world.

"I did meet one of Ava's neighbors, a nice fellow named Keegan Scott. Now he..." Janet says in an airy trance, "*was interesting.*"

The song lyrics from the previous night stir her heart with the sudden realization that she met Keegan while feeling uncertain, like a stranger in the early evening light. When their eyes met in the pale moonlight, it felt spontaneous, instinctive.

How many lives do we get to live? Janet wonders as she considers her married life on the East Coast with a twist of heartache.

She understands that memories of her late husband and the love that brightened her life will always be part of her deep inner being. But now, she was living with expectations of a future hope. The moment Keegan approached Janet on the patio, in the gentle breeze of a late summer evening, they were of the same world.

Weeks or maybe months from now, would she be contemplating their relationship, holding a showy red hibiscus flower while reciting, "he loves me, he loves me not, he loves me...?"

CHAPTER FIVE
BIG TECHNICOLOR CLOSE-UPS

J anet walks the lengthy stretch of corridor en route to her employer's bedroom, head lowered in thought, contemplating how this new job opportunity has re-defined her world. True, there is that long drive home every evening to the familiar urban landscape and cozy confines of her downtown studio apartment. Still, each new day as she enters Ava's sprawling lakeside estate, something moves her toward a future that feels intentional and purposeful. In addition, she has been asked to house-sit this weekend, which will be another new experience for Janet. It's a challenge working for Ava Fleming, she admits to herself, but then most things worth doing usually are.

Janet has grasped a few imperatives of her new job. *One*, that Ava requires a motivational speech or pep talk before the day's upcoming activities, and *two,* to offer daily assistance with clothing and shoe selection. Ava never changes handbags. She has one black leather Italian 'hobo'

Gucci bag that zips closed. Often, the bag is left unzipped and unattended on the glass case countertop in a retail boutique or abandoned in the corner of a dressing room. Janet has learned to keep her eye on Ava's handbag, one of the many details she must pay attention to.

Far from what the name *'hobo'* implies, Fiona said the purse came with a hefty $3,000 price tag. The bag's contents are usually visible: a cellophane packet of Kleenex, a light purple, pebbled-leather wallet, foil-wrapped butter rum toffee candies, and empty golden mylar candy wrappers.

Ava's wardrobe has been well-organized by the housekeeping staff. Encased behind floor-to-ceiling glass doors with brass antique door closures, Ava's garments and accessories are on full display, with an 'art museum' kind of vibe. Items that may have sentimental value, or are seldom worn, are showcased in the upper compartments of the glass closets: creamy satin, elbow-length gloves, an emerald green boa (St. Paddy's Day, perhaps?), and an assortment of dark-plumed hats resembling exotic birds in striking sustained poses. The garments are reminiscent of another era, bringing Ava's Hollywood parentage to mind. When the glass doors open, there is a leathery smell mixed with the lingering scent of expensive perfume clinging to slowly decaying fabric.

An entire room is dedicated to housing Ava's wardrobe: Janet's studio apartment would easily fit within the same space at least twice.

Clothes are organized by color and activity, carefully placed on padded satin hangers, and vertically aligned with Ava's lux leather size four shoes. Janet wonders how her own navy blue, utilitarian, *Easy Spirit* size ten shoes would look centered on the floor in one of the closets, and it makes her smile.

Despite Janet's own basic nondescript wardrobe, Ava seeks her advice each morning, then disagrees, wrinkling her nose in disgust, and selects something of her own choosing.

Whatever it takes, Janet says to herself with a shrug of resignation.

But before turning into Ava's bedroom suite, Janet's thoughts are interrupted by a sudden movement, a flash of bare arm, a disturbance in the vapid calm silence of floating molecules. Instead of turning into her employer's bedroom, she instinctively turns toward the blur of motion to the open door directly across the hall. Standing squarely in the middle of the hallway, she sees past the solid six-panel door into a closeted rectangular space with a view of her employer's semi-nude back, full frontal to an imposing titanium floor safe. Ava is partially hidden by the full height of the safe door, which is hinged on large steel plates. If a magician were present, with a wave of his black wand, Ava would vanish inside the tall silvery gray six-foot by three-foot vault and pop up in her bedroom under the covers of her peach satin bedspread. If this happened, the staff would be non-plussed as it would be just one more bewildering activity within Ava Fleming's illusory dwelling.

The door to the safe swings slowly open on its own, exposing more of Ava's back. Janet notices the exterior of the safe door with its polished chrome drop handle and mechanical dial, similar to what she had on her high school locker but looking secure to the point that once closed, the safe would be impenetrable. A dusting of morning light from an overhead skylight softens the enclosed space as Ava stands chest level to a velvet-lined drawer that has been pulled out. She appears mythical as a woodland nymph who has stumbled upon hidden treasure.

Ava pulls another velvet-lined drawer out above the first, and Janet sees a series of drawers within the safe. Ava does not see or hear Janet standing in the hallway as soft daylight pours over her. She appears to be at her spiritual oasis, fascinated by the otherworldly glow of brilliance emanating from the extended drawers. Pinpricks of piercing light float star-like above trays of black velvet from diamonds, precious stones, and chains of buttery gold, some chunky and others as delicate as the interlaced threads spun from a spider.

Janet knows she must respect her employer's privacy, but she is like the frenzied paparazzi that cannot turn away, so unexpected and disconnected from her own real world that she struggles to grasp the image before her. She wonders, is this the ghost web of the rich, to consider that some wants are not meant to be understood?

What is the point of all this jewelry, for instance?

Some things are so obvious. Like what would a person wish for if they could have anything at all? *Success? Friends? Wealth?* But here is the contradiction, Ava is a *philanthropist,* and her role as such is to be recognizably generous and moral. Shouldn't she be dedicating her time and resources to worthy causes? Or is her jewelry simply the result of being the offspring of Hollywood film stars? Of living a life of worldly luxuries and leisure.

Ava's parents, Sebastian and Beverly Rose Fleming raised their daughter in the lofty wake of a jet-set lifestyle.

They were movie stars, recognized and adored for their talent and glamorous good looks. Her mother's drawn-on over-arching eyebrows and red lacquered lips were then the height of fashion. It was the era of epic Hollywood productions, big Technicolor close-ups appearing on one enormous cinema screen designed to hold the audience captive. Ava's parents played their roles with suave sophistication and smoldering sexuality, reminding Janet of the late Hollywood actors Clark Gable and Vivian Leigh.

Grand, gilt-framed portraits of Ava's mother and father prominently displayed on the wall of Ava's home library seem to shift between past and present. In morning light, the portraits appear as relics, flashbacks of the past. But as evening subdues daylight, the images move into the realm of the mystical, existing as real-world physical entities. Colors are vivid and three-dimensional. It may have something to do with the antique brass picture lights angled 'just so' above the portraits, illuminating the actors as living beings with an aura of nobility. No matter. Janet views the portraits as animated and surreal. It seems that velvet ropes, the kind used in art galleries and theaters, are in order.

They are portraits to be expected of a leading lady and her leading man during Hollywood's golden era. Beverly Rose Fleming poised on a plum velvet fainting couch, waiting for the curtain to rise, wearing a billowing, breath-of-pink drop-shoulder evening gown accessorized with the softened luster of matching South Seas pearl necklace and earrings. One bare arm resting languidly by her side with the conspicuous dazzle of a heavy aquamarine diamond ring. A wisp of melancholy darkening the actress's face, adding a shadow of somber moodiness to the legendary star's expression. It is the identical resting face of her daughter, Ava.

In contrast, the father's portrait is bold and robust. Sebastian was known for his strong personality. He stands impatiently with one hand resting on the back of a formal ebony bone chair, his square jaw, dark hair, and strong features indicative of a scene-stealing actor. Sebastian Fleming came from a working-class background in the small town of Stirling, Minnesota. Janet was told that Sebastian had a ferocious work ethic that catapulted him to stardom, earning him a gold statuette for artistic excellence in cinematic achievements.

Could it then be said that all humans are essentially a DNA mix of each parent, rendering us a remix of our parent's attributes? Was Ava acting out the role she was assigned at birth a consequence of her glamorous, pampered upbringing?

Was it less privilege and more burden to be gossip-column fodder, to keep pace with the rich and famous? Ava was not particularly outgoing or well-spoken. Instead, she was wistful and often downcast. It must have been difficult for Ava to live from FADE IN to FADE OUT. Living from scene to scene, movie to movie. Watching her parents' larger-than-life world through the eyes of an insecure adolescent who remained half-hidden behind heavy velvet curtains and movie sets.

Without being detected, Janet stealthily turns, then stepping lightly, hurries down the hallway and back to her desk in the lower level of the home.

Within minutes, Ava's voice can be heard through the house intercom, asking Janet to come up.

Janet walks quickly from her desk, returning to the entrance of Ava's bedroom suite.

"You're driving me to Cassandra Crawford's home today. She's designed an important piece of jewelry for me," Ava says with an uncharacteristic edge of excitement.

Another piece of jewelry? Janet can't imagine why.

Ava was truly beautiful. She did not need to enhance her appearance with jewelry. Okay, she was exceptionally glamorous with diamonds, pearls, and gems, but shouldn't a philanthropist be less acquisitive? Janet decides to take the moral high road and considers Ava as someone she could lovingly guide to do and be better. Janet sees Ava as a project.

Jewelry designer Cassandra Crawford lives in an upscale neighborhood close to a park with mature landscaping and gently winding streets. The quiet well-spaced homes are thirty to forty years old, stately, solid, and separated by walls of dense shrubbery and hedges.

They call Cassandra from the car phone as they pull into her driveway, and soon she appears in the entryway of her home, looking sophisticated and humorless. She waves Ava in.

Janet squints, thinking she has seen Cassandra Crawford before. She recognizes the upsweep of raven hair, the smooth, straight nose, and the dramatic application of blood-red lipstick to accentuate her shapely mouth.

Yes! This is the woman in the red dress - from Sheila Livingston's party! This is the woman Maxwell disappeared with on the night of the party.

Ava turns to Janet, "You can return in one hour."

Apparently, Janet isn't welcome in Cassandra's home to see the custom-designed jewelry. It may be for security reasons or because Janet had been Maxwell's date, and Cassandra prefers to keep her distance.

Whatever the underlying reasons, Janet is relieved to have an hour of free time. They had passed a Starbucks coffee shop en route to Cassandra's home. Janet backtracks finds the corner coffee shop, parks the Mercedes out front, and strolls in to order a mocha latte. She spies a two-person table near the window, drags a wooden chair across the tile floor with a piercing scrape, and then quietly mouths "*Sorry*" to the person seated at an adjacent table. She settles in with her hot coffee drink and stares out the window in full view of Ava's car, with a watchful eye on the time.

Janet fully appreciates the pace and variety of her new job. Ava could certainly be demanding at times, but these unexpected moments of quiet reprieve allow her to catch her breath and experience a few moments of calm contentment.

After one hour, she returns for Ava but waits in the car another thirty minutes, trying to catch a glimpse of activity within the home. Unfortunately, Cassandra Crawford's expansive windows are heavily draped, and the exterior of her home is darkened by the proximity of brownish-black tree trunks and a leafy canopy hanging on low twisted branches. So, there is nothing to see.

Ava finally emerges, holding a pocket-sized brown box. She steps gingerly into the car, clutching her small possession. Ava removes the lid from the box as they drive away, revealing a rose gold necklace punctuated with a round amethyst stone pendant. The purple stone is undoubtedly eye-catching but looks costumey and fake to Janet.

"It was designed just for me," Ava whispers, looking down at the showy piece of boxed jewelry held on her lap.

Glancing sideways at her passenger, Janet senses that Ava views jewelry as the one thing that will bring her happiness. Finding the one precious thing she does not own, the one beautiful thing no one else has, *that's what Ava wants.*

"Is that your birthstone?" Janet asks politely, not knowing what else to say.

But Ava is lost in the moment and does not respond.

Janet is not interested in jewelry. It doesn't speak to her soul as it does to Ava's. She prefers her *Timex* watch, which lights up in the dark when a side button is pressed and keeps her punctual. It's not valuable, and she has no emotional attachment to her watch. It's simple and functional. In Janet's opinion, owning jewelry would be a burden. To insure it. To be constantly focused on its safekeeping. To draw unwanted attention to oneself. To possibly be targeted for a robbery. To coordinate the jewelry with clothing. Besides, she was too physically active to have chains hanging around her neck, rings on her fingers, and solid gold earrings dangling heavily from each ear, but then again, she wasn't a movie star or even the daughter of movie stars.

The idea of no jewelry or possessions makes Janet feel curiously free. Of expectations. Of the opinions of others. Of many things. Janet could risk being herself by dressing casually. Ava could not. Janet considers that Ava is caught in a spider web of pretentious glittering 'upper-class' bondage.

Ava swings open the car door before the car has come to a complete stop inside the garage and dangles one petite leg out the door of her enormous Mercedes.

Fiona, the housekeeper, stands at the partially open kitchen door smiling as Minka darts toward the car with an excited bark.

"Move! Move Minka!" Ava pleads. "Janet, please take this dog for a walk, will you?" Ava asks, holding her small treasure and trying to regain her balance. Then, gently, she pushes Minka away with one high-heeled foot before exiting the vehicle.

"Here, Minka! Let's put your leash on you," Janet says cheerfully to the excitable poodle.

It's a relief to be outside among the windswept trees and grass, the bold backdrop of nature's own treasures. This, Janet realizes, is what speaks to her heart. No half-ton titanium vault filled with diamond brooches and sparkly embellishments is necessary.

Once out of view, Janet unleashes Minka, and the poodle hightails it up the steep hill toward *Lady Slipper Lane.* At the top of the hill, the dog stops, looking back, waiting for Janet to catch up. The miniature poodle is so cute that Janet can't help but be amused by her fresh, unrestrained energy and spirit. She picks her up, feels the soft fluff of poodle curl against her cheek, and hugs the dog. But like a restless child, the dog wiggles away and wants to be set down to investigate the woods. Seeing a squirrel, she barks once, then makes a furious dash toward a distant tree.

Suddenly alarmed, Janet yells, "Minka!"

A moment later, the poodle is bounding back with a light-hearted bounce, her fluffy ears airborne. Minka sits at Janet's feet, panting as Janet attaches the dog's leash.

Rounding the corner of *Lady Slipper Lane*, a slow jogger appears. He is tall with dark blonde hair and shirtless, moving smoothly through the dappled afternoon light. Slightly ahead of the jogger, a husky German shepherd sets the pace, intently focused on the asphalt road before them.

"Hey, there!" yells the jogger. He holds his tee shirt with one hand and waves it above his head.

"Keegan Scott?" Janet responds.

"We meet again!" Keegan slows to a stop beside her.

"Is that your dog?" Janet asks.

"Ivan, come meet Janet," Keegan says, catching his breath. "Janet, this is Ivan Ivanovich, my faithful comrade. I gave him a Russian name. The name *Ivan* just seemed to suit him!" Keegan bends down and strokes the dog's back.

"He's beautiful and powerful, like a watchdog! Interesting name you gave him. Hey there Ivan, meet Minka. I believe Minka is also a Russian or Finnish name meaning friend," Janet says as she looks down adoringly at the poodle.

"What are you doing strolling *Lady Slipper Lane*?" Keegan asks.

"I'm walking Ava's pooch. I probably shouldn't have, but I removed her leash for just a moment," Janet motions to the pink patent leather leash studded with multi-colored stones. It stretches like a strip of candy button confectionery to the dog's collar. Shimmering in partial daylight, the leash is a stark contrast to the dark leafy foliage along the roadside.

"I decided a romp in the woods would be a nice change of pace from Ava's cool white marble hallways. Chasing a squirrel might be the most fun she's ever had. Thought I would liberate her for a playful half hour," Janet says, looking at Minka, then back to Keegan.

"If she'd like a change of scenery, bring her by my place! It's a lakeside property with woods and wildlife. Nice, but rustic. A far cry from Ava's palatial home," Keegan says with an encouraging grin. "I recall you saying you were curious about the neighborhood, am I right?"

At 47 years of age, Janet considers two things in her favor. First, she has a decent-sized vocabulary and breadth of knowledge, thanks in part to her work for a NY business magazine, and second, she is a sound judge of character. She now considers Keegan. His humor and light-hearted kindness, even toward Minka, impress her. He is kind of 'perfect'. Maybe too good to be true? *Is he married or involved?*

Keegan turns with interest toward Minka's leash. "Are these gemstones?" he asks, touching the shiny dangle of patent leather.

"I'm not sure," Janet answers, "I can't tell the difference between precious gemstones and department store knockoffs."

It's a long shot, but Janet's curiosity is piqued. "Do you know the jewelry designer, Cassandra Crawford, the woman at the party the night we met?"

"Yes, she's an acquaintance."

"If you don't mind me asking, what do you know about her?"

"She's a local girl. Once upon a time, a Miss Minnesota runner-up. Now married to that defense attorney, you may have heard of him, Nigel Blackstone. Famous for working on a jewelry heist case. It was quite a few years back. Why do you ask?"

"I've seen her a couple of times in the past few weeks, once at Sheila Livingston's party and today at her home." Careful not to offend Keegan, Janet stops herself before saying what she thinks: Cassandra strikes her as insincere and deceptive. "Just wondering," Janet says casually, looking away.

"Well, okay then," Keegan says lightly, "the mysteries of Cassandra Crawford-Blackstone..." His voice trails off.

Janet purposely changes the subject. "As it turns out, I've been asked to house-sit this weekend while Ava Fleming and her husband fly off to her late parent's Beverly Hills estate. So, I'll be in your lovely lakeside neighborhood all weekend!"

"Great!" says Keegan, his face lighting up. "Why not come over for dinner tonight? I was planning on cooking. You okay with Italian?"

Janet considers Keegan's invitation. His smooth, tanned skin glows with perspiration. He's not overly muscular but toned and very appealing. Laying a hand over her heart, she says with a spontaneous laugh, "Sure, I love Italian food! Just thinking of Garlic bread makes me hungry! You will have garlic bread?" she asks hopefully. "Italian food is so comforting! I must admit, I feel a little uneasy watching Ava's house for the weekend and would truly enjoy your company," she smiles. "I'm sure Ava won't mind. I'm allowed to take a dinner break while house-sitting, right?"

"Absolutely!" says Keegan. "Walk with me; I'll show you the way to my home."

Keegan's easygoing nature causes Janet to relax. Minka and Janet follow Keegan and Ivan Ivanovich, backtracking down *Lady Slipper Lane* toward a heavily paved road sloping to the shore of Diamond Lake. She hears the water slapping against the rocks, then sees the familiar sight of the sun-bleached wooden dock in Mariner's Bay. A jagged wooden sign identifies the road as *Hidden Cove.*

"I'm down there," Keegan says, pointing. "The A-frame near the beach."

Keegan's home is on a full-acre patch of native prairie flowers and grasses that morph into sand and rock near the shoreline. The property is adjacent to a forest of sugar maples and oak trees. Janet appreciates the radiant autumn colors and is impressed with the natural beauty and simplicity of the property.

"How in the world did you find such an idyllic location for your home?" she asks.

"Originally, it was my parent's lakeside cabin. They gifted it to me, and I've since remodeled."

"I'm guessing you enjoy your privacy?"

"At times, yes. It's a bit secluded. It will be nice to have your company this evening."

Janet glances at her watch, "I better head back."

"So, tonight then?" Keegan asks.

"Yes, tonight it is! Okay, if Minka tags along?"

"Yeah, sure. See you around seven?" Keegan asks, his blue eyes translucent in the sunlight.

Janet gives Keegan a friendly wave and turns, with Minka scampering at her heels.

CHAPTER SIX

A ROMANTIC GESTURE

J anet encounters both housekeepers, Sarah and Bonnie, just as they are leaving. Sarah turns to Janet as Bonnie looks on.

"We've heard you're house-sitting this weekend."

"I am," Janet answers.

"We set up the 'housekeeper's room' for you."

"I wasn't aware there was a housekeeper's room?" Janet responds.

"Well, that's what it was used for. There were a series of full-time housekeepers that lived in that room. It's the only bedroom with a lock on the door. The housekeeper's room is the fourth bedroom suite at the end of the hall."

"Okay. Thank you."

"Don't be startled if you hear noises during the night," Sarah adds. "The house is full of mechanical sounds and noises echoing off the lake. During winter months, shifts in the ice can cause the lake to boom like a cannon."

"Thanks for the warning," Janet says with a glance at Bonnie.

Raising her eyebrows, Bonnie gives Janet a false smile of encouragement and shrugs. The two housekeepers move toward the kitchen door, pass through the garage, and outside to the parking area where their nearly identical SUVs are parked side-by-side. Janet wonders why Sarah would mention unfamiliar noises. *Was she trying to frighten her?* Ava's home is secured with an alarm system, and the Diamond Lake police patrol regularly. So, there's really no reason to be fearful. Janet keeps her thoughts to herself and smiles pleasantly, "Have a nice weekend," she calls after them.

Fiona folds a dish towel in the kitchen and lays it near the sink. "Well, guess I'm off as well. Oh, forgot to mention that I made chocolate-dipped strawberries with crushed pecans for Ava. You might as well eat them, or they'll go to waste."

Janet's eyes light up, "Thanks, Fiona! I guarantee the strawberries will be devoured and enjoyed!"

Mindy and Elaine finish up in the lower-level office and soon follow the housekeepers and Fiona out the door. Janet watches through an oblong narrow pane glass window near the home's front entrance as the last car motors up the hill and out of sight.

Janet changes quickly into a soft blue fitted tee shirt, washed denim jeans, and sandals. She looks in the mirror and feels her stomach flutter. *Too casual?* She rummages through her overnight bag for her denim jacket. The vintage brooch she bought last week on an outing with Ava is pinned to the thick denim pocket. The large, leafy green shamrock brooch has an organic flare while still seeming stylish. She doesn't want to appear too bohemian. On the other hand, Keegan lives in a cabin, and anything more would be overkill. She runs a brush through her hair while taking several deep breaths to calm her nerves. It's only six p.m. She still has an hour before her dinner date with Keegan.

She takes the dish of strawberries from the refrigerator and places it on the counter, then stares at the strawberries. *Not enough.* She heads downstairs to the wine cellar and selects a bottle of Chianti. There's plenty to choose from, and this bottle seems like a mid-range red wine. It won't be missed. She then plays with the house alarm, keying in the code to lock the house and then unlock it. Minka looks up inquisitively, waiting motionless for Janet's next move.

Finally, they step into the garage, and Janet lifts the poodle's car seat from Ava's garage floor, placing it in the back seat of her Honda Accord. She straps Minka in with a safety harness, and the poodle is perched in the back seat of the car, looking forward. Janet runs back into the house to set the alarm, then dashes out to her vehicle during the five-minute interval she has to escape before setting off the alarm. Minka looks alert and attentive from her doggy booster seat.

"We're all set!" Janet says, adjusting and then looking in her rearview mirror at the poodle.

It's a short, pleasant drive to Keegan's home. Janet has her driver's side window down, and the air blowing through her car is saturated with the earthy fragrance of fresh lake water and damp autumn leaves. She pulls onto the grassy slope beside his cabin home and exits her vehicle, freeing Minka from the car seat harness. The poodle jumps onto the grass, then shakes her fluffy poodle hair with an air of satisfaction.

Janet grabs the bottle of red wine from the car's passenger side and Fiona's plated dessert, a rich and luscious contrast of ripe red strawberry and decadent chocolate, with a sprinkle of crushed pecan. She decides that Fiona's culinary skills are equal to those of any celebrity chef.

She walks the gradual slope, down and around to the lakeside entrance, which features an enormous semicircular span of wooden deck, then steps up a short stack of stairs with Minka close behind. A blue hammock swings lightly in the breeze, and Janet sees into the house through the sliding glass patio doors.

Holding a wooden spoon, Keegan waves at her from the kitchen. "Coming!" he hollers.

"No need, I got it!" Janet responds.

Holding the plate and bottle, she balances herself, then slides the partially opened glass patio door back with one foot. Minka scoots ahead, then pauses to look back.

"Go ahead, Minka," Janet urges. The dog hurries to sniff and greet Keegan, who then offers the poodle a bite-sized treat.

Keegan's home is more spacious inside than it appears from the exterior. A loft overlooking the main floor draws the eye up. The A-frame has high, triangular ceilings and rustic log cabin stylings. Unobstructed views of the lake and natural light flowing through the glass doors seamlessly transition between an indoor-outdoor experience. The great room is open and comfy with soft leather couches and a wall-mounted TV. A wood-burning stove fits snugly into a narrow corner of the room.

"Adorable! What a great place!" Janet exclaims, setting the wine and strawberries on a granite countertop.

"You brought dessert! Excellent! Chocolate-dipped strawberries are one of my favorites. And wine, too, thanks! Give me a moment," says Keegan, "just stirring in some fresh basil."

"Take your time; the sauce smells delish!"

A sloping pillar candle burns brightly in the center of an iron frame bistro table with a blue-stone top. World-famous tenor Luciano Pavarotti sings *Figaro,* which causes a giggly reaction from Janet.

"Thought we might listen to some opera with our linguine," Keegan says, raising an eyebrow.

"Nice touch," she says, still laughing.

The opera singer's clear, grandiose tones harmonize pleasingly in the background as opera music fills the room with a sweep of drama. The atmosphere is warm and intimate. A wave of pure happiness flows through Janet.

She wanders across the room to a log-built pine bookcase displaying a collection of pictures in metal frames and focuses her attention on a grainy 8x10 photograph in an antique silver frame. Examining it closely, she sees a group of young adults appearing jubilant, many hands together, holding a silver sailboat trophy high in the air. Front and center is a young boy with a wave of tousled hair.

One of the women is unmistakably a young Cassandra Crawford, and there are others. The picture includes Ava Fleming and, yes, even Maxwell! Janet is slightly alarmed but then considers the aloof, upper-class gentry of Diamond Lake, and it seems only natural that their paths would have crossed.

"I thought we might make our own pasta," Keegan announces.

Janet turns away from the bookcase.

"I've rolled out the dough, and we'll use the pasta machine. First, dust your hands with flour like this, then pass the pasta through the machine's rollers a few times until it's smooth. You game?"

"Absolutely! Sounds like fun."

Janet loves the idea of assisting Keegan in the kitchen. Soon, they are working side-by-side, lowering homemade pasta noodles into a stainless-steel stockpot of salted boiling water.

"Now we just wait several minutes for the pasta to cook," Keegan says, pouring them each a glass of Chianti.

"Here's to Diamond Lake," he adds, raising his glass to Janet, "where the women are strong, the men good-looking, and the children are above average."

"Hey! I've heard that line before! If this were Lake Wobegon, you'd be wearing quilted oven mitts and would have prepared a tuna casserole. Your Italian cooking and spices smell delish! I can hardly wait to taste the sauce. So, I propose another toast. Here's to my new friend and neighbor, Keegan, for his hospitality and flare for gracious living."

The wine captures reflective sparkles of flickering candlelight as they clink their glasses together.

Janet sips her wine, enjoying the full-bodied taste with a hint of spicy cinnamon. She feels a world away from Ava's opulent mansion of cool marble surfaces and empty, echoing hallways.

On the other hand, she really doesn't know much about Keegan. She's relying on her instincts and trusting they are taking her in the right direction.

After another sip of wine, Janet crosses back to the bookcase and points to the picture of Maxwell, Cassandra, and Ava.

"When was this picture taken?" she asks.

Keegan wanders over. "That's a picture of our Diamond Lake sailing regatta. Post-high school days for some and Middle School days for me. That's my uncle, Gerald Scott," Keegan says, pointing to the California beach boy look-alike at the group's center. "He taught me to sail. He's such a great guy! There's Maxwell, Cassandra, and Ava," Keegan says, pointing them out.

"Your uncle? I thought that was you!"

"No, I'm the small, shy blonde kid up front and center."

"How were you allowed to photo-bomb this picture?" Janet asks.

"Ava isn't a sailor. She doesn't even swim. I would sit with her while the others were sailing. We'd watch the sailboats glide smoothly across the lake and chat a bit. I was there to keep her company. Her parents sponsored the team. They were decent folks."

"So, you were friendly with Ava? Cassandra Crawford and Maxwell?"

"Well, in a way, yes. I was more of a tag-along. After all, I'm several years younger. Cassandra was friendly with Maxwell and a few of his friends. They were a close-knit group that worked well together and managed to win the competition."

Keegan is a delightful dinner host and adventurous cook, stirring in herbs from his garden. The atmosphere is casual and inviting. Simmering flavors of tomato sauce waft through the cabin, and the luminous glow of candlelight puts Janet in a warm, relaxed state of mind. Even Minka sighs with contentment as she lounges near the span of patio windows, her eyes partially open to keep tabs on a slumbering Ivan.

"So, tell me a little more about yourself," Janet says encouragingly.

Keegan motions to the bistro table, and they sit down to two steaming plates of linguine.

"Well...here's something of interest. This house was a very basic cottage when I took it over. My parents left me a few properties. That's how I spend my time now – doing renovations and repairs. I'm a retired pilot."

"You were a pilot! Why did you stop flying?"

"On a long trip to Tokyo, we were crossing the Pacific Ocean, and I decided thirteen hours was longer than I wanted to be on a plane. I had had enough. I'd been flying for twenty-three years. I put in my time and officially retired at age fifty."

"So, you never married?"

"Once. Many years ago. She was a local talent, an actress, and a model. As it turned out, we had different interests and went our separate ways. She married a money manager. After that, we lost touch."

"So, when you say different interests – you mean..."

Keegan answers matter-of-factually, "My parents belonged to a hoity-toity country club and lived an upper-class lifestyle. My dad, now passed, was a successful attorney but worked long hours. I didn't see much of him growing up. Guess I wanted something different for my life," Keegan pauses to sip his wine. "My young, impressionable wife became quite enamored with the jewelry, sprawling homes, and social climbing. I'm the down-to-earth outdoorsy type. I enjoy a cocktail party every now and then but prefer sailing and hiking."

Janet nods her head with interest as Keegan continues.

"She never wanted to miss a party. I like to travel when the mood hits me. As it turned out, we just wanted different things. What about you?" Keegan asks, twirling the linguine with his fork.

"When my husband passed away three years ago, I moved back to Minneapolis from New York, and I've been taking it a day at a time ever since." Janet rises, moving toward the kitchen, then brings the plate of chocolate-dipped strawberries back to the table.

"Delicious!" Keegan says, biting into and savoring the flavors of ripe fruit and smooth dark chocolate with pecans.

"Ava's cook made them just for us!" Janet says with a wink.

As they hug goodbye, it becomes a lingering kiss that sends a pleasant tingling sensation through Janet's body. Keegan is taller by several inches, but his warm embrace feels comfortable and natural. She feels the muscular strength of his shoulders as her hands glide smoothly over his back, and she feels him lean in, his kiss becoming fervent.

Janet pulls away reluctantly, "I better head back."

"So soon?" he asks.

"There will be other evenings," she says, feeling a jolt of warmth radiating through her body. "I hope," she adds.

They kiss again, one last time to say 'good night', and Janet feels more confident and calmer than when she first arrived.

Driving up the hill leading to her employer's mansion, Janet is alarmed when she sees a parked car near Ava's garage. It looks familiar. *Yes, it's Maxwell's car!* The red convertible Mercedes is shrouded in darkness beside a row of dense shrub trees. The black convertible top is up, and the vehicle appears to be sitting empty. She approaches the house, driving slowly, then flips on her high beams and feels for her cell phone, ready to dial Keegan, or the Diamond Lake police, if necessary. The automatic garage light sensors flick on, illuminating the spacious outdoor parking area. But before pulling into her parking space, she sees Maxwell seated on the iron garden bench as if waiting for her.

"What's up, Maxwell?" she asks, exiting her car and freeing Minka from the back seat safety harness while believing a calm and steady approach would work best in this situation.

"Is Ava gone for the weekend?" he asks.

Hesitant to answer any of Maxwell's questions, Janet responds, "Is there something you need?"

"It's okay if she's gone. I can wait. I guess. When will she be back?"

Janet feels uneasy offering any information to Maxwell and, against her better judgment, answers, "Monday."

Maxwell appears pale and thin under the harsh beam of direct outdoor light, and Janet wonders, with a flush of panic, what could possibly bring him here so late at night.

"And how are you doing?" Maxwell asks.

"Good!" Janet answers cheerfully, trying to end the conversation on a quick, upbeat note.

Janet wishes she had swapped dogs with Keegan. She would have Keegan's powerful dog, Ivan Ivanovich, and he would have Minka for all the reasons that were becoming more apparent by the minute.

"Mind if I come in for a while?" Maxwell asks.

"Actually, I do," Janet responds. "The house has a video recording of all movement and activity." Of course, it was a white lie, but she hoped this information would act as a deterrent.

"Huh! Never knew that..." Maxwell says suspiciously. "Tell Ava I stopped by then, will you?"

"Sure thing."

Janet stands uneasily beside the closed garage door. She waits until Maxwell gets in his car, drives down the slope, then up the steep hill, and out of sight before opening the side door with her house key and deactivating the alarm. Now safely inside Ava's home, she heads downstairs to her lower-level office. Minka follows her down the stairs and stretches out in a half-slumber on the threshold of her office doorway. She is seated at her computer, browsing emails, when she hears a noise, like a door rattling. She freezes. Minka sits up, ears perked.

Cautiously but with haste, Janet ascends the carpeted stairs two at a time and listens near the kitchen door. Nothing. She tiptoes to the front hall entrance and peeks through the narrow accent window beside the front entry door. She sees a spear of light. *Car headlights?*

The house phone rings, and she crosses the room, answering uncertainly.

"Ava Fleming residence, Janet speaking."

"Hi Janet, this is Officer Don Nelson. We received a call that the home alarm was tripped."

"Oh, that may have been me returning home from a dinner date. Sorry." Janet replies. "I'm new to this alarm system on and off stuff."

"Just following up on a call from the security company," says the Officer. I checked your entry doors, and they appear to be locked. Would you mind coming to the front door?"

Janet steps outside, and the officer nods. "Have a safe evening," he says, returning to his squad car. Slowly, diligently, the Diamond Lake police car moves past the grand front entrance of Ava's home, then away from the estate and up the hill.

"Good to know we're being looked after, right, Minka?" Janet says, looking down at the poodle, but more to comfort herself.

She double-checks that the house alarm is set and the red "armed" lights are blinking. Then calling it a night, heads down the long marble corridor to the furthest of the four bedrooms with Minka padding close behind. She slips into her nightgown as the poodle settles into her sheepskin doggy bed on the floor.

Janet steps over the dog and climbs onto a luxurious bounce of bedding and mattress. She snuggles between the lavender-scented bed sheets. Both Janet and the poodle fall quickly asleep.

Somewhere between dreaming and half-waking, she is startled by a noise, an echoing vibrational sound, like the low murmur of voices. Janet sits up in bed with her heart pounding. The room is dark, but she can see Minka's small soft body curled in on itself, sound asleep in the oval-shaped doggie bed, her sides expanding and contracting with rhythmic breaths. Janet focuses on the dog's slumbering posture and steady breaths as a point of concentration. She listens with all five senses and her sixth sense of intuition.

The water pipes? She wonders. *Do old pipes sound like this? Could it be one of the many house sounds Sarah, the housekeeper, had warned her of?*

Janet slips out of bed, careful not to disturb Minka or be detected by an intruder, and pulls on a short cotton terry knit robe, wrapping it protectively around herself. Quietly, slowly, she opens the bedroom door, hesitating momentarily when the lock on the door handle pops open with an audible click, then tiptoes warily a few feet down the hall. She stops.

In the shadowy darkness at the far end of the marble corridor, she sees what appears to be two standing figures or at least the hazy, half-formed mist of two beings. Unable to identify the forms as either 'male' or 'female', rather two entities that seem to have a floating kind of presence.

But she set the house alarm!

She cannot decide if what she is seeing is real or simply a blur of darkness in a shadowy corner.

Janet turns back to her room as quickly as possible and quietly locks the door behind her. *This can't be happening,* she says to herself.

Minka is still asleep! Wouldn't the dog wake up if there was a noise? An intruder?

Am I imagining this?

She grabs her cell phone, hesitant but ready to call the Diamond Lake police.

Was it simply the illusion of something floating in darkness?

Her thoughts trail off into self-doubt, and her body feels weak from the rush of adrenaline she has just experienced. She sits on the edge of the bed, cell phone in hand, motionless, concentrating, listening for another sound or some disturbance, but hears nothing. Still clutching her cell phone, she lays on the bed and pulls the down-filled comforter up and under her chin for added security.

Soon morning light is flooding the bedroom, and the dog yawns audibly. Minka needs to go outside, and Janet needs to feed her. Relieved that she and the poodle made it safely through the night, Janet unlocks her bedroom door and leads the little dog down the spacious hallway. The home looks bright, open, and undisturbed. She wonders what frightened her during the night. Was it the result of too much wine, chocolate, strawberries, and romance? Was it a water pipe? Or maybe even the housekeeper's suggestion that she would hear noises?

She heads toward the kitchen door, which leads out into the garage and then outdoors. But along the way notices the six-panel door to Ava's safe room standing partially open. She stops and gives the wooden door a gentle push. A delicate sparkle of silver chain catches her eye on the floor in front of the safe. Picking it up, she examines it. A weighty heart-shaped locket is attached to a loose tumble of silver chain. One side of the locket is inscribed with the word '*Forever*', and the other side is engraved with the silver etching of a single rose.

The locket clicks open to display two petite oval-shaped photos. One is a deep red rose, and the other is a picture of a young woman Janet does not recognize. Once fanned open, all four sides of the silver locket are revealed.

Turning the locket over in her hands, she wonders who the inscription *Forever* was intended for. A romantic gesture, no doubt. *Could this be the property of Ava's famous mother, Beverly Rose?* The miniature portrait may be a younger, fresher version of innocent Beverly Rose Fleming before fame and Hollywood glammed her up. And how did this piece of jewelry suddenly appear on the floor as if recently dropped?

Holding the necklace in her closed hand, she carefully reaches high, setting it in a tidy heap on top of the jewelry vault. The locket isn't extraordinary and has no gemstones embedded in the silver. It doesn't appear to have much value other than perhaps sentimental value. She pulls the heavy safe room door shut behind her and listens for the closing click.

Janet keys in the 'unlock' security code to turn the house alarm off as she prepares to take Minka out for her morning break. But once outside, from over the hill, she spies Maxwell's red Mercedes heading speedily toward her. She jumps aside as he pulls up next to her. He hops out of his car with urgency as though he is making a quick stop and has somewhere else that he needs to be.

"Oh crap," Janet groans, *"And he knows I'm alone."*

"One small favor," Maxwell says to Janet as he exits his vehicle. "I believe I left my wallet on a side table the other day while visiting Ava. Would you mind if I had a quick look around?"

"When were you here last?" Janet asks.

"Friday afternoon," Maxwell responds impatiently.

"I haven't seen your wallet on a side table, but I'll take a look. Which room did you say you left it in?"

"The sitting area next to the kitchen," Maxwell answers.

He shifts nervously from one leg to another, then bends down to ruffle the poodle's fluffy head. The miniature poodle has placed her two front paws on Maxwell's long leg hoping for attention. He gently pushes her away.

"Maybe just a look around the area I was seated in," Maxwell suggests to Janet. "I'll be quick. It's a Gucci, embossed black leather wallet."

Maxwell appears harmless enough in the softened morning daylight, but Janet knows he may or may not leave under protest.

"I'd prefer to look for the wallet myself because of the security cameras," Janet responds.

"Oh, for God's sake, Janet!" Maxwell says, suddenly irritated and disbelieving as he steps toward the house.

"I think you should leave now, Maxwell!"

He hesitates, looking into the garage, and sees that the kitchen door is wide open. Janet looks as well and suddenly intuits what he is considering. But before either of them can move, Keegan appears, jogging down the hill toward them with Ivan Ivanovich in the lead.

"Hey, Janet!" Keegan yells to her, waving hello.

"Thank you, God," Janet whispers, looking heavenward to the clear morning sky with a deep sigh of relief.

Minka runs toward Keegan's Shepard and prances excitedly around him.

"Keegan," Janet pleads, taking a few unsteady steps forward, "would you mind keeping Maxwell company while I run inside the house to retrieve an item *he may have* left on Ava's side table?"

"Sure thing," Keegan answers.

Janet feels immense gratitude for Keegan's perfectly timed appearance and feels her face heat with warmth. Then, before heading indoors, she gives Keegan a quick, darting glance to express her hidden thanks.

She overhears Keegan telling Maxwell of the new additions he's built onto his lakeside property.

Minutes later, Janet returns without Maxwell's wallet. "It's not here. Have you tried retracing your steps from before you lost the wallet?"

"Yes, Janet, that's why I'm here!" Maxwell answers with a sarcastic edge to his voice. Then, angry and disappointed, he turns toward his car, "You could at least let me look around the house. I would have easily spotted it."

"I'm sorry, Maxwell, but I've received specific instruction not to let anyone in the house while Ava and Richard are away (she lied). If I see it, I will call you. What's your phone number?"

Maxwell says nothing. He hops abruptly into his compact car and peals away with a loud screech, leaving a black smudge of tire rubber on the pink cobblestone drive.

"*Seriously?!*" Janet says, looking at Keegan in disbelief. "What's his problem?"

"I'm afraid Maxwell is used to getting his way," Keegan responds.

"Well, he better think again. Okay, if I borrow your dog for the weekend?" Janet asks, rolling her eyes and shaking her head.

Keegan looks protectively at his German shepherd.

"Just kidding," she adds without smiling.

Keegan straightens his posture, looking sympathetically at Janet. Then with a lighthearted smile, he shifts the mood and playfully asks, "How about a game of Frisbee? Just the four of us. You, me, Ivan, and Minka?"

CHAPTER SEVEN

FOREVER - BEVERLY ROSE

Keegan balances the lime green *Frisbee with* eyes focused on a distant sugar maple, a breathy flutter of fiery orange and yellow leaves.

Head up, alert, the German shepherd freezes in anticipation as the neon disc sails across Ava Fleming's expansive lawn. Ivan runs like a highly evolved predator. His front paws leave the ground as he leaps into the air with graceful agility, catching the *Frisbee* in his powerful jaws.

From a safe distance, the poodle looks on, her body tense with heightened interest. Too intimidated to join in. Living vicariously through the noble heroics of the German shepherd.

"Poor Minka! She wishes she could jump and catch like Ivan!" Janet laughs.

Elaine drives up as Keegan playfully tugs at the *Frisbee* clenched between his dog's teeth. She swings her car into its usual parking spot and eases out of her midsize black Volkswagen Jetta.

"Hi, Elaine!" Janet says, startled to see Ava's bookkeeper on this quiet Saturday morning. Then motioning toward him, "This is Keegan Scott. Ava's neighbor. We met the night of Sheila Livingston's party."

For a moment, Elaine looks curiously at Keegan, then back to Janet.

"Oh yes, Keegan! Nice to meet you," Elaine says with a strained smile as she extends her slender hand. "Looks like you two are enjoying this perfect autumn morning."

Elaine's graceful silhouette reminds Janet of an aging platinum-haired ballerina. Seated at her desk under the incandescent glow of office light, Elaine doesn't appear quite so translucent and colorless as now, at 10 a.m., poised on the pink-hued cobblestone pavers of Ava Fleming's driveway.

Then, with a half-turn, she directs her attention to Janet directly. "Can I have a word with you?"

"Sure, what's up?"

Elaine steps in closer, her back to Keegan as she speaks in a confidential tone. "Richard called to let me know that he and Ava will be delayed a day or two. Can you house-sit a few days longer?"

Janet watches Keegan as he jogs across the yard toward his German shepherd.

"I guess," Janet answers, "but why didn't Richard call me directly?"

"I've been Ava's bookkeeper for eight years. Richard knows me."

"Makes sense," Janet agrees slowly.

"We're heading home!" Keegan calls back to Janet. "Catch you later!"

Janet waves to Keegan. His toned physique distracts her. His muscular calves and well-proportioned leg muscles: tanned and glistening.

"You have my number?" Janet shouts across the vast lawn to his retreating image.

Keegan smiles and gives Janet a 'thumbs up' response, then turns to his dog. "Come, Ivan!"

Ivan regains possession of the *Frisbee*. Then, together, the two of them jog up the steep hill, disappearing into the bucolic landscape of trees and scattered sunlight.

Janet turns to Elaine, "Elaine, I'm glad you're here. Would you mind stepping inside for a moment? There's something I found this morning that I want to show you."

As they approach the safe room, the door to the closet housing Ava's jewelry vault stands slightly ajar. Minka, the poodle, looks on with an impatient whine.

"What's wrong, Minka?" Janet says, looking curiously at the poodle. Then to Elaine, "How odd, I closed this door tight less than an hour ago."

"Hmmm," Elaine says, "Maybe the latch is loose?"

"But I heard it click shut."

Elaine jiggles the heavy brass knob anchored to the solid six-panel door, then steps back. Cautiously, Janet pushes the door completely open. She steps inside the 'safe' room and reaches up, groping for the locket she placed on top of the jewelry vault earlier. But instead of feeling a singular item, she feels two objects. She lowers her arm slowly as she examines the objects in her hand.

"I found the silver locket on the floor earlier, but what is this?" They both stare as she displays in the palm of her hand not only the locket but a curlicued brass key resembling a treble clef attached to a tiny fluff of silken blue tassel.

After a thoughtful pause, Elaine says, "I'm guessing the key belongs to Ava's *Rococo* nightstand. The antique styling and decorative detail."

"Should we leave it where we found it or place it on the nightstand?" Janet asks.

Elaine crosses the hall to Ava's bedroom. Janet follows. They stand together before the antique gold nightstand. It has the soft, worn aesthetic of a well-loved family heirloom. Elaine takes the key from Janet and holds it at arm's length matching it with focused concentration to the keyhole-shaped opening in the top drawer.

"We could at least find out if the key fits," Janet says, urging the bookkeeper on.

Elaine leans in, positioning the key in the keyhole. It's a perfect fit, but when she attempts to remove the key, the drawer pulls open with the key still intact. They stare silently at the drawer's contents: a cream-colored envelope with the name *Maxwell* scrawled across it in faded mauve ink.

"I guess this would be a good time to tell you that Maxwell has been by the house a few times since Friday," Janet says softly and now, somewhat baffled. "He says he lost his wallet somewhere in the house."

"Maxwell stopped by the house?" Elaine asks with a flush of color reddening her cheeks. "He was here Friday afternoon! You and Ava were gone. I wonder if Sarah said something to him about Ava and Richard leaving for the weekend?" She closes the drawer. "That Sarah – she's a troublemaker."

"Sarah...the housekeeper?" Janet asks with an incredulous stare. "Why would she tell Maxwell I was here alone, house-sitting?! I had a hunch about her. Always sneering when she sees me pass by."

Just then, Ava's bedside telephone rings. Startled, Janet fumbles for the receiver, "Fleming residence," she says, her voice an octave too high.

"Oh, hello, Janet," Ava replies in a subdued tone. "Did Elaine deliver the message that Richard and I will be spending a few additional nights here in Beverly Hills?"

"Yes! In fact, Elaine is with me now. She was kind enough to drop by and tell me in person."

"How is everything going?" Then without waiting for a response, Ava continues, "I'm so tired of Beverly Hills. So much paperwork and so many meetings. It's exhausting. I want to come home."

"We'll be waiting for you," Janet says, trying her best to sound sympathetic.

She glances at Elaine, then back at the *Rococo* nightstand. It seemed as good a time as any to report on Maxwell. "By the way, your friend Maxwell dropped by. Says he left something behind last time he was visiting."

"Oh?" says Ava, followed by a brief moment of silence. "I wonder if he's after that letter I mentioned. I was going to give him the letter but then couldn't remember where I had placed it."

Janet hesitates. She couldn't tell Ava what she and Elaine had discovered without sounding like snoops, but she could tell Ava what she found on the 'safe' room floor.

"Actually, one other thing, I found a silver heart-shaped locket lying on the floor. It's inscribed with the word '*Forever*', and when you open the locket, there is the miniature of a red rose and a beautiful young woman."

Janet examines the necklace in the palm of her hand, then sets it carefully next to the key on the nightstand.

"Yes! I remember that necklace! *You found it?! Lying where?*"

The thought of being in Ava's 'safe room' suddenly strikes Janet as unsettling. "On the floor, outside your bedroom," she lies.

"Amazing! I thought that necklace was lost 'forever'!" Ava laughs, delighted at the irony of her pun.

"It was a prop necklace my mother kept from one of her earlier movies titled, **Forever**. She let me wear the necklace for the movie premiere. I wore it with a beautiful dark blue dress puffed out with petticoats. I felt like a six-year-old princess. Even my father said how lovely I looked when I twirled to show off my sparkly new dress with the locket. What wonderful memories..." Ava's voice trails off. "You found the necklace on the floor? How odd."

Janet and Elaine stand quietly, looking at the tangle of silver chain and locket lying on Ava's nightstand.

"Also, there was a key. We placed it on your bedside table until you decide where we should leave it."

"Oh," Ava says suddenly, remembering, "I think I put the letter to Maxwell back in my mother's *Rococo* nightstand. That's where I found it! Look now; see if it's still there."

Elaine overhears the entire conversation. She looks at Janet and shrugs. Janet places the key back in the keyhole, and the wooden drawer pulls easily open.

"Yes...there is an envelope with Maxwell's name written on it," Janet reports to her employer, feigning surprise.

"Is the letter sealed?" Ava asks.

"Just barely. Do you want me to open it?"

Ava pauses, "Well... maybe it *would* be best if you read it to me before Maxwell sees it, or I forget about that letter once again."

Janet removes the letter from the limp, cream-colored envelope as Elaine quietly leans in. After a quick scan, she notices some mention of Ava's personality that might be too sensitive to read over the phone. Janet hesitates before asking, "Would you like me to just read the opening paragraph as an introduction to the letter?"

"No, no," Ava demands, "read the entire letter, or what's the point!"

Janet steadies her hand, suddenly noticing how dry her mouth has become.

September 1961 - Dear sweet Maxwell, how often I have thought of you throughout the years and the blessing of your friendship with our beautiful daughter, Ava.

As I write this letter, you are an up-and-coming professional golfer with the good fortune of your athletic ability and an innate feel for the game of golf. It is amazing to watch your marvelous talents and abilities unfold, but I would be remiss if I did not celebrate how you fanned the flame in others: how you drew forth the highest and best in our daughter, Ava, making her path brighter.

Sebastian and I have often remarked on your youthful exuberance and positivity. You were there for her when our careers took us to Africa and India. You kept the home fires burning, including our daughter in your circle of friends and social activities.

Most difficult of all was Ava's slow recovery from the head injury due to the Blue Ribbon Equestrian Center accident. Ava was inconsolable when she learned that her horse had to be euthanized due to the fall. Although several years have since passed, our daughter would not have recovered as quickly without your encouragement. Because of you, she became more self-assured: joining first the tennis club and then the Diamond Lake Yacht Club, where she overcame her fear of water.

It's not easy growing up the only child of working actors, but the additional trauma of Ava's brain injury was difficult beyond words. Your devotion to our daughter during those years touched our hearts, and we will forever be grateful. Thank you!

I also wish to thank you for the many lovely cards and notes of affection you left for me. I understand how glamorous the life of a movie star must seem, but in truth, everything truly meaningful happens off-stage, out of the spotlight. It is loving relationships that carry us through difficult situations and strengthen our resolve to carry on. A true friend is a treasure, a jewel.

On this note of gratitude, I wish to give you a token of my heartfelt appreciation. May you continue to create an extraordinary life

for yourself, and always remember to cele-
brate the greatest gift of all – friendship.
With deepest gratitude, Beverly Rose

"Well!" Ava says, interrupting her assistant, "That's quite a letter! First of all, Maxwell was lucky to have *me* as a friend! I was the popular one. I was the one with friends. Maxwell didn't even have a girlfriend! And the Yacht Club – *ha*! Sunburn and horseflies, that's what I remember! Sitting on a rickety old dock watching sailors skim the waters of Diamond Lake was boring! My mother had it wrong! And furthermore, tennis never was my thing!"

"There's a bit more," Janet adds.

"I've heard enough!" Ava says. "I have to go; Richard just walked into the room!"

The phone clicks off.

"What do you think?" Janet asks Elaine.

"I think Ava is furious that Maxwell now has claim to a valuable piece of her mother's estate jewelry if that's, in fact, the gift being offered. Of course, Ava doesn't mind writing Maxwell a check, but a piece of her mother's jewelry will not sit well with Ava. As I'm sure you've noticed, she's very attached to her jewelry, inherited or otherwise." Elaine pauses. "I've often thought her jewelry was a substitute for love."

Janet nods in agreement.

"Also, the letter makes Ava sound like a rather unpopular young lady that Maxwell took pity on," Janet adds.

"True, the letter does make Maxwell sound heroic," Elaine says, looking past Janet to the span of patio doors facing the lake, "but from what I've gathered, Maxwell is now an aging ex-pro golfer who's been engaged to a succession of rich widows and divorcees."

This was the most information Elaine had ever shared with Janet. The floodgates were open.

Encouraged, Janet continues, "What is he now, like an aging gigolo?"

"Well, that's a little extreme. More like a shady opportunist," Elaine answers with a wry smile.

"It sounds like Maxwell befriended Ava because he had a boyhood crush on her mother, Beverly Rose Fleming," Janet adds.

Elaine's voice rises in pitch, "And who wouldn't? Ava's mother was a classic beauty!"

"Why wouldn't this gift of jewelry be in Beverly Rose's will, and why wouldn't Maxwell have known of it sooner?"

"I'm not sure, but it would be interesting to find out. Perhaps Ava's mother stashed the letter in a drawer, then forgot about it?"

"But where *is* the gift Ava's mother promised to Maxwell, and *what exactly* is it?" Janet asks, contemplating the letter in her hands. "Hmm . . . this is interesting . . . there's a hand-scrawled note on the bottom of the page that says, 'file Transfer on Death Deed to Maxwell H.'.

Janet looks at Elaine, who shakes her head doubtfully.

"Seems this situation is a puzzle best left for Ava and her attorney to resolve. Let the professionals put the pieces together," Elaine advises.

Janet folds the letter and prudently returns it to the envelope. She sets the letter to Maxwell back inside the drawer, but as she attempts to close the drawer, something catches. She pulls the drawer open to its full extension. Everything seems in order. She bends to one knee, looking inside the lower half of the cabinet. The interior space seems too shallow for the frame of the cabinet. *False wall?* she wonders.

Looking up, she finds another envelope stuck to the bottom of the drawer. Janet slides the drawer back then forward to loosen the envelope, but it catches and crumples like a wave.

"What the...another envelope! What do I do with this envelope?" Janet asks with a bark of laughter.

"Who is it addressed to?" Elaine asks.

"No one!"

Elaine glances quickly at her watch. Her eyes widen. "I don't know...just place it under Maxwell's letter," Elaine says as she fiddles with her watch. "I really must get going, Janet. Will you be okay staying here a few extra days?"

Janet suddenly feels drained. She rises to her feet, wondering if she can push past her fears. She briefly looks down in thought before answering.

"To be honest, late last night, I could have sworn I saw some kind of shadowy presence in the hallway... outside the safe room."

Elaine becomes motionless. She lowers her head, then answers quietly, "Well, that wouldn't be the first time..."

Janet laughs in astonishment. "What are you suggesting? That the house is haunted?"

Elaine says nothing. She's a bookkeeper with a logical approach to life. "There have been rumors..." she finally answers, looking away.

"A spirit? In the house? But *who*?"

Elaine hesitates again, speaking softly, "My guess would be Ava's father, Sebastian. Maybe he's here to redeem himself and help his daughter. I've heard stories of how strict he was with Ava. He also wanted to control his wife's career. Sebastian was a perfectionist who could be demanding and confrontational."

"How did they deal with his behavior?" Janet asks.

"As I understand it, his wife was intimidated by her husband's behavior. She was, at times, fearful. Beverly Rose's greatest successes were her roles in romantic dramas. Rumor had it Sebastian was convinced a succession of mediocre films was damaging her career."

"Wow. I did not know this. The things we learn...how sad for Beverly Rose," Janet murmurs.

She slumps into the satiny slipper chair near the foot of the bed. "I'm truly sorry for Beverly Rose Fleming and Ava, but what am I supposed to do, house-sit with her father's ghost hovering in the next room?!"

"You said yourself that it may have been nothing more than your imagination. Set the house alarm and call if you need me or the Diamond Lake police. I'd offer to stay the night with you, but I'm watching my grandchildren this weekend. I've got to get back; my daughter's waiting for me."

Janet rises from the chair, facing Elaine, "What would you say if another person stayed with me? Because of the Maxwell situation and all?"

Elaine looks doubtful. "Why? Who are you considering?"

"Ava's neighbor, Keegan. He invited me to his home and prepared a wonderful dinner. I enjoy his company. Also, Keegan is an old acquaintance of Ava's. He could sleep in one of the guest bedrooms, couldn't he?"

Elaine looks down at the nightstand, pausing as she touches the key, smoothing the attached silken blue tassel with her fingertips. "Did he agree to spend the night?"

"I haven't asked him yet..."

Elaine looks directly at Janet. "You might want to consider that someone other than *me* might find out if Keegan spends the night. *I wouldn't* invite him over, but then I'm not you. I get it, big scary house. You're the house-sitter. You're in charge. I would advise you to have him gone by the time the housekeepers arrive on Monday morning if you decide to have him stay."

Janet looks past Elaine as if staring into the future for an overlong moment. Her mind races through the possibilities with a looming sense of uncertainty.

Would Keegan even accept her overnight invitation? Would this invitation (in some way) make Keegan feel uncomfortable?

Or would something go wrong? Would she eventually ask herself, 'What was I thinking?'

No, no, she says. She stops herself mid-thought. *I won't even go there...*

Instead, they would laugh and snuggle and spend time getting to know each other better.

"Thanks, Elaine, for your advice. I'll walk out with you."

And with that, Janet knew exactly what she was going to do.

CHAPTER EIGHT

THEATRICAL VIBES

When Keegan calls later that afternoon, Janet proposes that he stop by. She doesn't mention the overnight idea. Instead, she'll ask him later if they both feel comfortable. He can spend the night in one of the guest bedrooms if he prefers.

"I would, but I'm getting together this evening with a few friends on the other side of the lake," Keegan explains. "We're meeting at *The Lodge* to watch the Twins game."

"Oh." Janet settles heavily into a swivel bar stool beside the kitchen counter.

"I could come over after the game if you like. Are you nervous about spending another night alone in Ava's house?" Keegan asks with a laugh.

Janet fidgets in the swivel chair, turning it side-to-side with one foot at the base. "Actually, I am. There are some situations that are unsettling. Maxwell is one of them."

"Don't worry about Maxwell. He would never do

anything to jeopardize his friendship with Ava."

"Oh, I wouldn't be so sure of that," Janet responds with a hard half-turn of the chair. "Also, Ava's house is noisy. Lots of unfamiliar sounds."

"If you like, I could drop Ivan off, then stop back later. Ivan's a great watchdog."

Janet stops turning in the chair, and sits up straight. "I would love that!"

"Are you sure Ava won't mind me and Ivan stopping by?"

Janet shifts uncomfortably, recalling Elaine's cautionary advice. "No, it's okay," she says, feeling a flush of guilt warming her face, "I mentioned it to Elaine."

Later that evening, Keegan drops off Ivan. "Take good care of our girl!" Keegan says to his dog. Ivan barks as Keegan drives away, up the hill and out of sight.

"He'll be back, Ivan," Janet says, smoothing the shiny black and tan fur behind the dog's ears. *Such a beautiful animal; I wonder why Ava doesn't own a watchdog like Ivan. He might be better than a house alarm.* She then feels bad for thinking less of Ava's diminutive poodle and picks her up, holding her in a hug as the dog leans against her chest, then tilts her head up to lick Janet's face.

Now, with both dogs and Keegan's anticipated late evening visit, Janet feels more at ease. She decides to watch a movie. But before heading downstairs to the theater room, she pops a bag of microwave popcorn that smells up the kitchen with its artificial blend of buttery flavors. The dogs follow her and the aroma of popped corn down the stairs. The deep flame-red tone of the theater room feels a bit garish for Janet's Midwestern taste, but the heavy velvet of the rich crimson curtains and red leather loungers give the room a distinct theatrical vibe.

Janet powers on the remote control. A small projector lowers from the ceiling with a mechanical hum, and slowly an image fills the screen spanning the length and breadth of the far wall. The loungers are generously proportioned and tiered on a platform to comfortably seat an audience of twelve.

The poodle jumps up and snuggles into the seat beside Janet, but Ivan, the shepherd, lumbers down the carpeted aisle steps and stretches his full muscular length across the floor in front of the screen, finally settling in with an audible sigh.

She returns to the kitchen, filling two doggy bowls with water, but when she returns, the poodle has her moist, black nose buried in the bag of popcorn. "No! No!" she cries. But it's too late, and the dog begins roughly licking the stiff, greasy insides of the bag.

She heads back upstairs to the kitchen to dump the crumpled bag of popcorn. The popcorn is uneaten, she notices, but has lost its appeal. She decides to pour herself a full glass of chilled New Zealand Sauvignon Blanc instead and selects a Waterford wine glass with an oversized bowl and deep V plunge resembling a tulip. The floral cut pattern creates a tactile experience as she cups the glass and slender stem with both hands, swirling the wine inside the glass for effect.

Ahh...peace at last... she murmurs while settling back into the reclining leather lounger. She begins flipping through a selection of cable channels and is delighted to come across the Classic Awards Movie channel. The layering of dark and light tones cast a grayish pall over the set and actors, presenting them as grainy two-dimensional images, like a vintage photograph. A small print blurb pops down when she presses the program info button. *'Forever'* is a Hollywood classic film starring Beverly Rose Fleming and Sebastian Fleming. 1946.'

With keen interest, Janet leans forward in her seat and watches Beverly Rose Fleming move about in an old southern-style, dimly lit bedroom. As the camera angles in for a close-up, the movie star's green, almond-shaped eyes glisten with tears. Janet is mesmerized by the actress's graceful movements. Beverly Rose, in a floor-sweeping satin gown that billows over her voluptuous movie-star curves.

Tinkling, single-note piano keys play in the background as a precursor to some heightened drama. One window, open to the cold stare of moonlight, is loosely framed by linen drapes blowing raggedly into the room. Beverly Rose crosses to the open window in a state of utter fatigue or despair (it is unclear which) and pushes down on the heavy wooden-framed window. It requires a great deal of effort for her to close the window, and the action seems to deplete her strength. The restless night air has tousled her soft curls, which fall in bouncy waves around her sad, oval-shaped face. Turning away from the window, she sees a tall, silhouetted man blocking the bedroom doorway.

The orchestral music intensifies. The star gasps, covering her mouth with one hand while holding her suddenly disheveled gown in a tight-fisted grip with the other. Stepping away, now with her back to the wall, the only thing separating her from the shadowy figure across the room is a four-poster Queen Anne bed.

"*Yikes!*" Janet shouts at the screen.

Both dogs look up as she takes a deep drink from her glass of wine, which has formed cool droplets of moisture over the crystal. The background music grows shrill and sharp as the mood shifts from despair to terror. Then, from the darkened doorway, the actor steps forward, revealing it to be her long-lost fiancé, Sebastian, who went missing in action during WWII.

He moves toward her, then stands silent, searching the actress' face for a reaction. She appears disoriented as he looks into her eyes, then to her pale throat. Finally, the music switches to that of a weeping violin, and there it is - *the necklace* — the heart-shaped locket, which the actress suddenly clutches in disbelief.

"You're still wearing it," the fiancé says in a hoarse whisper to Beverly Rose with misting eyes.

"Yes, I have lived with but a whisper of hope."

"My rose! My love!" the actor exclaims, moving passionately toward her. "You are mine, now and forever."

"That's the necklace! That's the necklace I found this morning!" Janet exclaims with a shrill of excitement.

Alarmed, Ivan rises from the floor and barks. The poodle follows suit with a sharp, noisy snap of a bark.

"Sorry guys," Janet says, leaning over to stroke Minka's fluffy head.

Wow! Last night could have been a scene from this Hollywood movie. The starlet's lover appears in a shadowy corner of the room. They passionately reunite. The necklace is a gift of promise to return to his betrothed before going off to war. Of course, it's all a little fuzzy, but could it be that there are two spirits in Ava's home re-living a scene from this movie?

Janet had heard of early Italian Renaissance theater in

which the actors would play the same characters their entire lives.

Could it be along those lines? Could the spirits be living that same day, those same characters over and over again, as some unresolved life event?

For a moment, Janet considers calling her mother to discuss this, but it's late, and she feels a little tipsy from the wine. She snuggles deep into the comfy chair, extends the leg rest, and lets her head relax upon the softness of leather.

She wakes with a start, realizing she has dropped the remote, and is surprised to see both dogs missing from the room. As she searches beneath her chair for the remote control, she hears the faintest groan of a closing door. The TV host is introducing the next movie in the lineup, *"For this Saturday evening..."*

Janet quickly finds the remote on the floor and lowers the volume, listening intently for other suspicious sounds. She leans forward in the lounger, looking down the lengthy stretch of corridor leading to Ava's library. Over-sized African ceremonial masks hang from the walls. Their exaggerated expressions: straw plaits of hair, the black gash of a mouth, and surprised eyes outlined in red paint are hardly reassuring. The corridor is a tunnel of diminishing light that narrows into blackness. She understands that the masks represent some of Ava's worldwide travels. Still, she wonders why an interior decorator would choose objects once used to frighten tribal enemies as wall hangings in a windowless lower-level hallway.

She looks behind her and up the stairway, flinching when the automated chair has a squeaky electronic reaction to the collapsing leg rest extension. Retrieving her wine glass from the floor, she notices her hand is trembling. She quickly sobers up.

What happened to the dogs? Could it be Keegan? But how would he have gotten in?

She hadn't set the house alarm for the evening, thinking this would be something to do after Keegan arrived. Janet was sure all the doors were secured, having double-checked each entry point earlier in the evening. Including the patio doors, she counted seventeen doors in all.

She inhales and exhales purposefully, slowly, to regain her composure. Cautiously, she ascends the soft carpeted stairway to the home's upper level, but still no dogs. She heads down the white marble hallway toward the bedrooms, but not before glancing out the narrow-facing window on the circular drive. She hears Minka whimpering, then sees Ava's closed bedroom door. Her throat is so constricted that she can barely swallow.

Janet tiptoes past Ava's bedroom door to the farthest guest bedroom down the corridor - *her room* - to retrieve her cell phone. Why she didn't have it with her annoys her, *"Shit!"* she says under her breath, digging into her purse. She scrolls through her contacts for the Diamond Lake police, which she had programmed into her flip phone earlier. The phone glows in her hand with a faint artificial green light. Her thumb poised above the "OK" button.

Then, returning to the area just outside Ava's bedroom, she puts her ear to the door. Nothing. Slowly, she turns the doorknob and cautiously taps the door open with one foot, holding the cell phone like intergalactic weaponry.

The poodle sticks her nose in the crack of the partially opened door, then wiggles through. Janet opens the door, taking in Ava's grand bedroom suite with a sweeping glance, the lofty vaulted ceiling and broad expanse of carpet. The king-sized bed with satin-tufted headboard, custom nightstands with matching French table lamps, and a peach pastel slipper chair near the foot of the bed. Her eye moves seamlessly across the soft color palette, resting at the far end of the room, near the fully draped patio doors.

Though the room appears unoccupied, she feels the residual energy of some intense drama or activity that came moments before. It is the eerie feel of an empty stage following the actor's exit.

Janet dials the number on her phone and hears, "Diamond Lake Police."

"Yes, hello. Janet Kelly, calling from the home of Ava Fleming," she responds in a strained voice. "Thirteen Diamond Lake Point, would you swing by for a house check?"

"Is there a problem?"

"No. Well, I'm not sure. I'm house-sitting the Fleming residence this weekend. I'm here alone, and yet I've heard some disturbing noises such as doors opening and closing..."

"We'll send out Officer Ryan," the Dispatcher answers.

The police were especially attentive to the celebrity residents living in the Diamond Lake community, and she now considers what the housekeepers told her, that the Diamond Lake police were well-acquainted with Ava's numerous late-night false alarm phone calls.

Suddenly, Janet catches a glimpse of movement from

the corner of her eye.

She sees the curtain at the far end of the room move: as though a body were hiding behind its weighty folds. The drapes cover an enormous span of patio doors and floor-to-ceiling windows that open to a concrete terrace and grassy embankment of lawn that slopes to the rocky shore of Diamond Lake.

She holds her breath while cautiously closing Ava's bedroom door with an even, steady motion as if she has seen nothing. Then waits outside for the Diamond Lake police squad car with her heart pounding.

When she returns to Ava's bedroom with police officer Ryan, the patio door is partially open. The drape pulled back. Officer Ryan opens the patio door wider, shining his flashlight across the cement terrace and grass. Two yellow points light up the darkness, and the officer asks, "Is this your dog?"

"Oh my God, yes! Come Ivan!" she hollers from behind the officer, but her voice is lost in the nearby sound of water lapping over the rocky shoreline. She runs outside to retrieve Keegan's dog.

"This is so strange," she tells the officer when she returns with Ivan, "I fell asleep downstairs in the theater room, and when I awoke, both dogs were gone. The poodle was in this room with the door closed. Also, how did this patio door open? How did the German shepherd get outside?"

"Was your house alarm activated?"

"No, I've been waiting for a friend to stop by. I have his dog, Ivan. I intended to turn the alarm 'on' after his arrival."

Janet now wonders if the movement behind the

curtain could have been Ivan, but it still doesn't explain the opened patio door and Ava's closed bedroom door.

"I passed a car on Ladyslipper Lane, heading away from the Fleming estate. What kind of car does your friend drive?"

"I'm not sure..." she says with hesitation. They head back outside as the outdoor sensor lights flick on. The officer sweeps the beam of his flashlight over the entire parking area and beyond into the dense row of shrub trees.

"Whose car is this?" the officer asks.

"That's my car."

"I passed a fast-moving sporty red car with a black convertible roof on Ladyslipper Lane. Does that sound like anyone you might know?"

"Maxwell!" Janet says angrily, her body tensing.

"Is that your friend?"

"He's not my friend! He's Ava Fleming's friend. I don't know what he would be doing here uninvited and unannounced."

"I suggest you turn your house alarm on after I leave and keep your phone with you. In a few hours, I'll send a squad car to patrol the area outside the home again."

Janet looks from the officer to the road climbing the dark hill away from Ava's estate. "Yes, I would very much appreciate that. Thank you, officer."

CHAPTER NINE

A PASSING RESEMBLANCE

J anet inhales the cool night air, taking a moment to
simply stand and be still. A sudden breeze stirs her
dark, shoulder-length hair. She smooths it back into
place, watching as the police squad car moves slowly up
the hill with its spotlight directed into a haphazard
interlacing of twisted black trees.

Thank God for the Diamond Lake police! she
murmurs, exhaling a small amount of relief. The poodle
and German shepherd linger by the door, eyes on Janet,
waiting to follow her back into the house.

With a hunch that the break-in was, in fact, Maxwell,
Janet returns to Ava's bedroom, crossing to the large span
of lake-facing patio windows and doors. She pushes the
vertical door handle against the metal frame, listening to
the quiet knock of metal on metal. The patio door is now
locked and secure. Then turning her attention to Ava's

nightstand, she notices the blue-tasseled Rococo key.

Is this where she left it?

With all the heightened drama, her memory is questionable, at best. She wants to take a second look at the letter from Ava's mother to Maxwell but finds it has been carelessly placed inside the linen-colored envelope.

Was this her own doing? Had she hastily, carelessly, inserted the letter only halfway into the envelope, then placed it back in the drawer?

Every detail now feels suspicious and confusing.

Why can't I remember? Stress? The wine? This house? And what am I to make of that crinkled, watery gray envelope beneath Maxwell's letter? What's the significance of that?

Janet steps toward the open drawer, tentatively lifting the unmarked envelope for a closer look.

Who would even know if I read it?

She turns the envelope over in her hands, still uncertain.

Hadn't Ava asked me to read Maxwell's letter just this morning? So, knowing more might be in my and Ava's best interest.

Several dried rose petals tumble lightly onto the bedroom carpet as she withdraws papers from the envelope.

A chorus of bells suddenly fills the home with a waterfall of musical tones. With a knee-jerk reaction, Janet hastily folds the papers, returning them to the envelope. She slides the envelope beneath Maxwell's letter and quickly closes the drawer. Then seeing the scattering of rose petals, she scoops them from the floor and sets them near the table lamp.

Hurrying to the home's front entrance, she peers through the narrow, vertical entryway window. She sees Keegan gazing off toward the outdoor parking area, dressed effortlessly in light khaki pants and a dark short-sleeved polo shirt. The polo shirt fits snugly, and the fabric band circling his upper arms draws attention to his toned biceps. Janet feels her heart beat a little faster.

Opening the front door with energetic cheerfulness, she greets him with "*Finally!*" and can hardly believe this is the first word out of her mouth.

Janet feels her face grow warm. Keegan steps forward and gives her a gentle kiss on the lips as she tastes the sweetness of malt liquor and bitter hops.

"Please come in!" she offers with a dramatic arm sweep.

"Thank you," he replies, taking an unsteady step into the grand foyer. "I parked next to your Honda. Do you think that will start any rumors?"

Was that nothing more than a faltering step, or did Keegan just drive intoxicated halfway around Diamond Lake?

Feeling suddenly cautious, she wonders about his judgment, then considers her own alcoholic tendencies as of late. She considers commenting on the perils and consequences of drunk driving, then slowly dismisses it as he straightens up and takes a few sober steps toward her.

"Rumors? Why, whatever do you mean, sir?" she says, trying her best to sound in character as the aging Southern belle, Blanche DuBois.

Keegan laughs. Then with a curious glance and a wink adds, "You haven't told me of your other suitors. Maxwell, for instance?"

"Maxwell?" Janet asks with annoyance, her tone suddenly serious.

"I saw him earlier this evening at the *Lodge*. He mentioned you. Told me you were alone this weekend at Ava's."

Janet feels her pulse race as she reaches for the entryway table, steadying herself lightly on the cool gray surface with her fingertips. She feels a sense of desperation that comes with helplessness. *Should she tell Keegan what she thinks of Maxwell, or would she come off as judgmental without the stone-cold facts to back her?*

But before Janet can respond, Ivan appears in the entryway, tail-wagging. Still flustered and unable to articulate an immediate response, Janet decides to give Keegan the benefit of the doubt. *Was Keegan reacting to Maxwell's interest in her? Had Keegan downed a few extra drinks this evening for courage?* Although she wasn't happy about it, it did seem a logical explanation.

"Hey there, Ivan! How's my boy?" Keegan asks.

Ivan barks in a seeming conversation. Keegan bends to greet his dog with one long gentle stroke along the dog's back. Ivan moves closer to Keegan and then sits.

"Wait here; I have a treat for us and Ivan. Give me just a minute. It's in my car."

"Can I pour you a glass of our non-alcoholic champagne, described as lusty, bubbly, and invigorating?

"Did you just describe yourself?"

Janet responds with a nervous laugh.

"No beer?" Keegan asks.

"Sorry. No beer in this home. A fresh floral sparkling wine is the best I can do."

"Sounds great!" he answers, looking over his shoulder

at Janet. He pats his thigh, and Ivan rises to follow Keegan out the door.

Peering inside the industrial-sized stainless-steel refrigerator, Janet reaches first for a small bowl of freshly cubed cantaloupe. She turns, setting the bowl on the granite kitchen countertop, then removes the thin film of Saran Wrap clinging to the orangey flesh of the fruit.

Suddenly, becoming acutely aware of another presence in the room, Janet looks up.

At the far end of the kitchen, near the pantry door, a sparkling silvery-blue concentration of darting, densely active particles form a vertical tower, an iridescent presence. The entity begins moving directly toward Janet, then past her; it almost seems through her! The moment is too astonishing to comprehend fully. She feels light-headed as a flush of adrenaline tingles through her body. She then turns to see that the entity has vanished.

Had she just encountered a... ghost, a spirit? Or what?

"For real," Janet says quietly to herself in a half-whisper. "This house *is* haunted."

Suddenly, spiraling through her imagination is the darker thought of spending another night alone in this home of eerie encounters with what may well be an entourage of spirits.

Please, Keegan, stay the night!

Keegan returns with two white foam, take-out food containers. He sets one on the marble kitchen floor for his dog, "De-boned chicken breast for Ivan," he says as the dog eagerly lowers his head into the white box, then places the other larger container on the kitchen counter, "and spicy chicken wings in barbeque sauce for us!"

He stoops down low beside his dog, then deftly slides a slender slice of white chicken meat from Ivan's boxed meal. "And a morsel for you, madam!" Keegan says, turning on the balls of his feet toward Minka. The poodle cocks her head to one side, approaches, sniffs, then cautiously nibbles at the treat Keegan has offered.

Keegan's companionable nature causes a shift in the atmosphere, and Janet feels, now, more than ever, a desperate sense of gratitude for his presence.

Would Keegan even believe her if she shared the bizarre events of this evening, or would he be frightened off?

She wants to present herself as the cheerful hostess and possibly more, but at the very least, she would like to appear *sane.*

With nerve endings still tingling, Janet asks, "How was your evening? Did you have fun?"

"It was great! The Twins won! Let's celebrate!"

Janet indicates the bowl of cantaloupe, "I can add blueberries?"

Keegan nods. Janet plates the fruit, spooning on the plump blueberries. Then, reaching again into the refrigerator, she moves a few food items aside and pulls forward a gold-labeled bottle of Non-alcoholic Sparkling Brut.

"Let me get that for you," Keegan offers.

"No, no, it's okay. I got this. I worked catering and waitress jobs during my college years. This will give me a chance to show off!"

She unwinds the wire cage from the top of the bottle, then pulls at the embedded cork with all her strength. The tugging focuses her energy, and as the cork pops, she feels the built-up tension of this day release and fly across the room with the cork. She lets out a wild whoop as Keegan applauds her. Non-alcoholic sparkling wine bubbles out of the bottle and into the Waterford wine goblets.

"Can't find the fluted Champagne glasses," she shrugs, handing him a glass.

Keegan looks at Janet, his eyes the color of calm water with reflections of gray sky, "To us!" he says, clinking his glass against hers. Janet gulps down half her glass of sparkling bubbly despite an earlier resolve to remain in control. Well...*it is non-alcoholic*, she reminds herself.

Keegan steps forward, curving his drinking arm partially around her shoulder while pulling her toward him with his free arm. Caught off guard, Janet steps back, laughing at the impromptu gesture. She feels his glass lightly touch the bare skin at the nape of her neck as a small trickle of sparkling wine races down her spine.

"I'm so sorry. Did I just spill my drink on you?" he asks.

"Yeah," she says, looking up sheepishly, "I must confess I was just thinking of what I told Maxwell the other day, that the house is armed with indoor and outdoor surveillance cameras."

"Is it?" Keegan asks.

"Nah.." she answers, with a kiss.

As he pulls her close, Janet sneaks a quick look past Keegan's shoulder, confirming the room's emptiness. She leans into the strength of his body, the security of his physical presence, enjoying the slow, deepening kiss: a mouth-filling sensation of his warm lips and tongue mixing with the citrusy flavor of sparkling wine.

With eyes closed, she says softly, "So glad you're here."

*You have **no idea** how glad I am!* Janet thinks to herself.

Janet pulls away and takes a step back.

"Would you care to join me in Ava's theater room for a private screening?" she winks, interlocking his fingers loosely between hers.

"Sure. I'm intrigued! You lead the way," he answers, grabbing both glasses of bubbly wine.

Janet returns the cantaloupe and blueberries to the refrigerator, "We'll eat this later, for dessert...with whipped cream!"

She nabs the gold-labeled bottle of sparkling wine and container of chicken wings.

They settle into the side-by-side red leather loungers, playing with the leg extensions and electronic seat adjustments like two teenagers at a movie theater. The dogs have followed them downstairs and casually stretch out: Ivan, below the screening area, and Minka, inconspicuous, near a swivel chair.

"I didn't know Ava had a theater room, but I should have guessed it," Keegan says.

"Why? What do you mean? Have you been in Ava's home before?" Janet asks, aiming the TV remote at the screen to power the entertainment system back on.

"Oh, yes. For a few of her evening soirees years ago and then one other time last summer. She didn't offer a house tour, though." Keegan looks around, distracted by the campy flamboyance of the room. "This home feels like a throwback to the golden age of Hollywood. It's *so* Ava Fleming and her parents!"

Keegan takes a slow drink, then continues. "I was here last summer with Maxwell. We stopped by to drop off a brooch or necklace. Something to do with jewelry."

"Why would Maxwell have a piece of Ava's jewelry?" Janet asks with a sharp turn of her head.

"Cassandra Crawford repaired a necklace clasp for Ava. Something along those lines."

Keegan pauses again to sip his sparkling wine and select a meaty chicken wing from the foam container.

"It was just a chance encounter. One summer morning, I stopped by the coffee shop with Ivan after our morning run, and there was Maxwell. We hadn't seen each other in a while, and he asked how the renovations were coming along on my lake home, so rather than explain, I invited him back to my place for a look. With Ivan in the back seat, we stopped first at Ava's to drop off the necklace. I was just along for the ride but then invited into her home."

"So, I have to ask," Janet pauses, "are Maxwell and Cassandra a couple?"

"Oh, some people believe that."

"What do you believe?"

"I've heard the rumors, but Cassandra is a married woman. Maybe it's just an understanding between Maxwell and Cassandra. They have a history, you know. Cassandra and Maxwell go way back to high school."

Even after a night at *The Lodge* with friends and a few drinks apparently consumed, Keegan appears subdued and rational.

"What about you?" Janet asks. "Did you enjoy growing up around Diamond Lake?"

"I did! I was on the swim team, and a great swimming beach is on this side of the lake. My uncle Gerald's home is just minutes from here. My parent's home was on the other side of the lake near the boat landing. No swimming there."

Janet nods with understanding and is about to ask more about his family when they both hear a heavy thud, like a body falling from the floor above.

"Did you hear that?" Janet asks, sitting up and muting the sound.

Ivan rises from his sprawled-out position on the floor and barks. The sound of his bark makes the sudden stillness of the room seem more pronounced.

"It's okay, Ivan. Was that from upstairs?" Keegan asks.

Janet holds the muted remote control in a frozen pose, and they both look up toward the ceiling as if able to direct their hearing to the floor above.

Suddenly remembering that she had not yet set the house alarm, Janet lowers her voice to a raspy whisper, "I better check upstairs. And... I need to set the house alarm again to keep us safe."

"Does that mean I'm locked in for the night?" Keegan asks, lifting one eyebrow suggestively.

Janet is struck by the ease with which Keegan responds and wonders if his nonchalance is because this is still somewhat in his neck of the woods, and unexplained sounds are to be expected. Either way, his manner of easiness is only moderately reassuring.

"Where's the poodle?" Keegan asks.

"Over there, behind the chair," she motions, "I'm guessing she's a wee bit hard of hearing or sound asleep."

"Oh, I didn't realize...I thought it might be the poodle knocking something over...I better come up with you."

"I was hoping you'd say that!"

Both dogs follow Janet and Keegan up the stairs. Ivan,

with bounding strides, and Minka, with short, scampering steps.

They enter the kitchen. It appears exactly as they left it. The spoons and Saran Wrap still on the counter, the room illuminated with the icy dazzle of the elaborate hanging crystal chandelier. They turn their attention to the white marble hallway leading to the guest rooms, but nothing appears out of the ordinary.

"I have a hunch," Janet says, turning toward a secluded wing of the home reserved for elegant gatherings and dining.

Minka stands immediately in front of Janet. "This dog is going to trip me! I'll slide her into the powder room for a moment." Janet gently guides Minka into the entryway powder room, closing the door behind her. Then, together, Keegan and Janet enter a linear arrangement of softly lit rooms, with Ivan following.

The first formal area is an elongated space complimented with circular, side-by-side crystal dining tables resting on milky white floating swan pedestals. Adjacent to the dining tables, an interior wall of blue-gold Tiffany glass doors conceals a dignified and sizable liquor cabinet. Other walls of the room are decorated in gigantic undulating splashes of contemporary artwork, and there is a six-foot metal wall sculpture with a bronze plaque titled '*Vibrations*'.

Even with the bodacious artwork and watery-colored glass doors, the room feels as though life has been sucked out of it. A suffocating dryness permeates the air, rendering it almost unbreathable.

Janet had seen this room during daylight hours, sparkling in dazzling sunlight with a cool, open airiness.

But now, at night, although orderly and physically unchanged, the room feels compressed, and it has a dizzying effect on her, throwing off her balance. The massive floor-to-ceiling windows overlooking the lake present bewildering, oblique reflections of the interior.

They continue into the second room, passing a glossy black Steinway piano with a raised lid against a white sandstone fireplace.

The final room, an informal dining area, a more intimate space, octagonal in shape with floor-to-ceiling windows, juts out directly over the darkened waters of Diamond Lake like the helm of a ship. The room, unlit and shrouded in shadow, is partially obscured by its polygon of various angles.

Then, from several feet away, they both see it. Positioned behind the circular granite-stone dining table, looking dapper in a crimson velvet smoking jacket with black lapels and black bow tie, is a gentleman holding a cigarette as if waiting for a light.

Keegan and Janet stand in stunned silence. Suddenly the stranger moves, or rather glides, from behind the dining table, and they see that the lower half of his body is nothing more than a trailing mist, a thin curling vapor of smoke. Though animated with life, the spirit is curiously without facial expression. Instead, he has a face, but his features are out-of-focus, as though too much light is passing through him.

Then, as easily as the spirit appeared, it rises and evaporates through an outside wall.

"What was that?!" Keegan asks in amazement. They stand motionless in paralyzing astonishment.

Janet lightly touches Keegan's arm. "Was that who I

think it was?" she asks.

"Why? Who are you thinking?" Keegan asks with an expression of utter disbelief.

"Ava's father, Sebastian Fleming?"

"Possibly."

"Did you recognize him?"

"I couldn't make out his face. It was blurred."

Janet nods her head slowly in acceptance. "I'm almost afraid to ask, but would you go with me to look in Ava's bedroom?"

"Why?"

"I'm wondering if that's where the noise, the thud we heard, came from."

"Maybe we should just pack up and spend the night at my place?" Keegan suggests looking suspiciously behind them. "We could lock up Ava's house, set the alarm, and let the spirits have the house to themselves."

"Come back in the morning?" Janet asks.

"Exactly. When the house is less haunted," he answers with obvious sarcasm.

Frowning, Janet runs her hands through her hair. She can't just leave. She looks beyond Keegan and sees Ivan at attention, gazing curiously toward them. She's supposed to house-sit, which means *stay here - overnight*. She considers Keegan's offer, her mind racing.

"Before we go, would you take a look in Ava's bedroom with me?" she asks again.

"Why? What are you looking for?"

"I'm not really sure. An open door or window? The reason for that *thud* we heard earlier. What clues would a ghost leave behind?"

"There are others?" Keegan asks with a jolt of surprise.

With a slight grimace, Janet shrugs her shoulders.

They retrace their steps, with Janet leading the way through the formal living and entertaining areas, then down the seemingly endless hallway toward Ava's bedroom without speaking. Janet stops cold and gasps. Keegan sidesteps to peer around her.

Ava's patio door is once again partially open, and a flow of late-night air has filled the room with a damp chill. The narrow top drawer of the nightstand is half-open. Janet crosses the room and pulls the drawer to its full extension, searching for the two letters she placed there earlier. She finds both envelopes shoved carelessly to the back of the drawer, and when she lifts Maxwell's letter out, she sees that it has been handled and is now smudged with ashy-gray fingerprints.

"Maybe we should call the police," Keegan suggests.

"I haven't told you of my earlier scare this evening. I called the Diamond Lake police about an hour before you arrived. The officer who came to the house promised to patrol the property overnight. I know he will. He seemed very reliable and tough, like an ex-military guy."

"What frightened you?" Keegan asks.

"This patio door. Open again. Who or what is opening it and why?"

"Are you sure that it's locking?"

"Yes!"

Keegan closes the door, locks it, then jiggles the locked door by the handle. He pulls, and the door catches once. He pulls again, harder this time, and the door slides open.

"A broken lock," Keegan says. "You can put a piece of wood in there to secure it."

After a pause, Janet says, "I got it!" She disappears

inside Ava's extensive wardrobe area and emerges with one aluminum trekking pole. *Property of Canyon Ranch* is printed in black lettering along the pole.

"See if this fits," she says, handing the pole to Keegan, "The height is adjustable; you just turn the pole from the middle."

"What exactly is this?" he asks, examining the object in his hand.

"It's a trekking pole used to keep your balance on hiking trails."

"I realize that, but is this 'stolen property' from *Canyon Ranch*?" Keegan asks, reading the label with a slow smile.

"Never mind!" Janet scolds.

Keegan wedges the trekking pole along the metal glide strip of the patio door: adjusting the height of the pole for a perfect fit. He is momentarily silent, then straightens up, looking directly at Janet, carefully weighing his words before asking, "Ever heard of a benevolent spirit? Here to help in some way?"

"Is that what you think is happening?" asks Janet.

"Well, no. A ghost, for instance, wouldn't open the patio door. On the other hand, if the fellow in the tux was Sebastian...I mean...I don't know. Ava's parents were good people. They loved their only daughter. Maybe they're trying to communicate something if their spirits are still around."

"I did think of that. *A spirit* or several spirits trying to communicate with or encourage us? I *do believe* in another dimension of existence; I just didn't think we'd be formally introduced!"

Janet sighs audibly, smoothing back her tangle of hair

with both hands. She has no intention of shirking her responsibilities but also no desire to spend the night alone in this house. Her job as Ava's assistant, *or whatever title she was assigned*, is still new and somewhat undefined. No one has yet discussed her recent performance, but she feels that she is being scrutinized. She briefly considers Sarah, the housekeeper, with her snarly, half-hidden disapproving side looks.

Janet takes a hesitant step toward Keegan before asking, "Would you be willing to spend the night with me...*here*?"

"Oh, Janet. I'm guessing we'd be much more comfortable and relaxed at my place," Keegan answers.

"True...but they are just apparitions. Ghosts that vanish easily into thin air. What if we sleep in the same room to feel safe?" Janet asks with pleading eyes.

"Our first night together in a haunted mansion would be *unforgettable*, but I don't think that's what Nat King Cole had in mind when he sang that song."

Janet feels her mood lighten, then does a double take as she observes Keegan frowning in concentration. She follows his gaze and sees him looking past her toward their slender, pale reflections in Ava's lakeside patio doors.

"Is someone out there?" Janet asks, turning to Keegan.

CHAPTER TEN

WHAT TRULY MATTERS

Keegan steps closer to the patio door as a waning misshapen moon wobbles milky light over Ava Fleming's backyard, casting pale light upon the narrow concrete terrace and sloping embankment of darkly jeweled lawn.

"What the..." Janet says with a sudden gasp, "Who is that!?"

"Maxwell?!" Keegan asks, somewhat baffled.

There, wandering like a lone wolf in the moonlight, is Maxwell. Instinctively, Maxwell turns his attention toward the ambient light flowing through Ava's glass patio doors and waves. Moonlight captures the glint and gleam of a silvery object he holds high for Keegan and Janet to see.

"Looks like Maxwell, dangling a set of keys!" Janet says, craning her neck and stepping forward next to Keegan.

Keegan bends toward the broken patio door, removing the trekking pole against Janet's muttered protests, and opens it wide.

"Hey, Maxwell," Keegan asks nonchalantly, "whatcha got there?"

"Your house keys, apparently. You left them at *The Lodge*," Maxwell replies with an exaggerated smile, walking toward the house.

Maxwell steps up and through the open patio door, then hands the keys to Keegan.

"Thanks! Was there a reason you came to this patio door rather than the front door?" Keegan asks.

"Well, I happen to know this patio door has been broken for some time. So, I thought I would just pop in and leave the keys on Ava's kitchen counter without interrupting the two of you," Maxwell says with a hint of betrayal in his voice.

"Why would you think you were interrupting us?" Janet asks, feeling a jolt of anger pulse through her body.

"When I entered the house, I heard the two of you talking downstairs and had second thoughts. Also, a police officer is outside right now checking out my car, and I think I might be in a bit of a *'situation'*."

Maxwell looks reluctant and meek, hoping to gain a small amount of sympathy from his audience of two.

"I hope you realize how suspicious this all sounds to us, Maxwell," Janet responds.

"Well, it's true! I stopped by to drop off Keegan's keys," Maxwell says defensively. "Also, who are you to be pointing a finger, Janet? You told me the house was monitored with surveillance cameras inside and out, and yet here you are with Keegan! Kind of hurtful, Janet. I thought we had an understanding."

"No, Maxwell. No understanding," Janet says flatly, shaking her head. "I think you have other reasons for being here tonight," she adds, suddenly buoyed with confidence.

"Such as what?" Maxwell responds.

"Ava's jewelry," she answers.

"Oh please, I'm no thief! And... if you're referring to the jewelry vault, Ava's '*secret code*' has been the same for years. It's her birthday or some combination thereof. I'm surprised you haven't figured that out yet, Janet."

Upon reflection, it was true, Janet thought. Ava did have difficulty remembering numbers. She could barely remember her home address and zip code and had a habit of glancing sideways at Janet to confirm that she had stated it correctly to the sales clerks.

"So, it was you that came in earlier and took a fall?" Keegan asks.

"Yes."

"Why didn't you leave the keys on the counter as planned?"

After a thoughtful pause, Maxwell replies, "I actually thought I saw someone in the hallway. He...or whatever...caught me off guard. When I turned to leave, I stumbled and fell to the floor before I reached the patio door. It felt...almost...as though I had been pushed."

"Did you see anyone?" Janet asks.

"Not sure. It all happened so quickly, maybe a round face, blurred as though with a soft-glow filter? I don't know! I realize how unbelievable this all sounds, but...whatever or whoever it was startled me!" Maxwell adds.

Janet and Keegan exchange a look of understanding and surprise just as the front doorbell rings.

"That's probably the officer," Janet says. "You two better come with me, so the officer can see that everything is copacetic."

"Look, Janet, before you answer the door, you might as well know I'm looking for something that belongs to me...something I've been promised. I know about the letter from Ava's mother. I know it's in the nightstand," Maxwell says, motioning to the Rococo piece of furniture next to Ava's bed, "but did you know there's more to that nightstand than meets the eye?"

"Whatever do you mean?" Janet asks slowly with obvious skepticism.

"Ava told Cassandra she remembers her mother telling stories of hidden treasure and secret spaces within the nightstand. She believes Ava's mother was sharing more than a bedtime story with her daughter. However, when Cassandra suggested this to Ava, she quickly dismissed it."

Janet's mind races back to a recent memory of Ava sharing a story on one of their daily outings. Janet was driving the silver Mercedes, and Ava seemed distracted by the scenery but could recite a story that seemed fresh in her mind — a tale of a narrow escape from a foreign land and a family secret. Janet thought Ava was recounting a television episode or a movie she had recently seen, so she didn't pay close attention. Then, rather abruptly, Ava stopped talking, returning her attention to the scenery whizzing past her passenger-side window.

Maxwell continues, "We are guessing this is how the letter from Ava's mother appeared. It floated through a secret interior wall."

"I better answer the door," Janet says with sudden urgency.

Maxwell and Keegan follow Janet out of the bedroom and down the hallway to the front door. Along the way, she considers that a police report will not reflect well on her house-sitting assignment, especially since she had invited Keegan to spend the night, and now, despite her prejudices, she is intrigued by Maxwell's story.

"Hello, again, Ms. Kelly, and who have we here?"

"Hello, officer. These are my two friends, Maxwell and Keegan."

"Hello, officer. Maxwell Hemingway, the third here!" Maxwell says, lightly stepping forward with a forced smile. "The red Mercedes convertible belongs to me, and this is my friend..."

"Good evening, officer." Keegan interrupts Maxwell with a firm nod. "Keegan Scott, pleased to meet you, and the other car, the Jeep Cherokee, is mine."

"Well, yes, this matches the information I received from dispatch," the officer says, referring to his hand-held notepad. "I called in the plates, and your names identify the cars in the driveway as yours. Janet, you identified the Honda Accord as belonging to you, which also checks out. Do you gentlemen have identification? May I see your driver's license?"

The men tug at their back pockets for IDs under the officer's watchful eye.

"Thank you. Gentlemen, would you please step outside while I speak with Ms. Kelly?"

Keegan and Maxwell comply as the officer closes the door behind them.

"So, Janet, you're telling me these two individuals are your friends?"

"Yes, officer, they are."

"I believe you told me earlier that Maxwell Hemingway was 'no friend of yours'," the police officer says, clicking his pen with a curious look at Janet.

"I did say that, officer, but Maxwell dropped off house keys for my overnight guest, and now, all is well. I apologize for somewhat of an overreaction earlier this evening."

The officer straightens up. His leather belt, holstered gun, and flashlight squeak and swoosh as the weight of the items adjusts to his movements. A call comes through the radio positioned on the police officer's shoulder, and he turns his head, remarking to the dispatcher that he is at the Fleming house number 13 Diamond Lake Point.

"10/4," the radio dispatcher answers back.

"I'm sorry again for the earlier false alarm. I'm okay now..." Janet says to the officer.

The officer gives Janet a doubtful but resigned nod. "Okay. It all checks out," he says, inviting the two men back into the house. "Let us know if you need anything else."

Distracted by the static on his radio, the officer turns away and gives Janet a quick half-wave before leaving the doorstep.

Janet locks the front door and then sees Keegan and Maxwell several steps ahead. The three of them gather in Ava's bedroom, forming a half-circle around the nightstand.

"Hmm, mm... hidden treasure," Keegan coos softly.

"Cassandra believes Ava's parents (for mysterious reasons) kept a secret hidden within the nightstand," Maxwell says.

"I was under the impression that Ava's memories were vague," Janet adds.

"*All* of Ava's memories *are vague*," Maxwell says with a hint of exasperation, "that's why we have to help her make sense of them."

"What's stopping Ava from disassembling the nightstand and removing the false walls to satisfy her curiosity? We all know how Ava would delight in a treasure hunt," Janet proposes.

"We believe Ava is afraid of disturbing the interior of the nightstand. A kind of superstitious fear somehow interwoven through her mother's bedtime stories of hidden treasure. I thought together we could persuade Ava to investigate the possibilities at least," Maxwell explains.

"But why would Ava need our help?" Janet asks.

"There is a chance that Ava would richly benefit from whatever is hidden within the nightstand, and Cassandra's husband is an attorney, who would be happy to represent Ava in any case," Maxwell answers a little too quickly.

Janet considers the possibility of some financial benefit to Cassandra's husband, Cassandra, and Maxwell as she looks away to face the patio windows. Then, shifting her thoughts adds, "Why on earth would Ava trust me, the new girl?"

Maxwell pauses before answering. He follows Janet's gaze, "She doesn't necessarily have to know if we knock on the wooden cabinet, say, find a hollow sound? You might even suggest to Ava the possibility of a false wall."

"Sounds innocent enough," Keegan adds with a shrug, looking from one to the other.

Janet turns and looks disapprovingly from Keegan to Maxwell. "Seriously?! This is an invasion of my employer's privacy!"

"She's right," Keegan says evenly. "It is wrong to snoop."

"Sorry, Maxwell, but nothing will be resolved tonight," Janet adds.

Maxwell flashes a cold smile of insincerity, refusing to respond to Janet's comment, then abruptly turns his back on her. "C'mon Keegan. You're leaving with me, right?"

Janet looks wide-eyed at Keegan.

"Give me a minute, Maxwell. I'll meet you out front."

"Oh, you're not staying?" Janet asks, unable to hide her disappointment from Keegan after Maxwell has left the room.

"I'll follow Maxwell in my car just a short distance to be sure he's gone," Keegan answers. "You know Maxwell; he'll tell Ava some story about us or come back late tonight just to spite you."

"You're probably right. So, you'll be back?"

"Yeah, I'll be back in five minutes; you have my dog," Keegan answers with a playful laugh.

They kiss and hold each other briefly before Janet escorts Keegan to the front hall entrance, where Ivan and Minka have chosen to sprawl out. The dogs yawn, rising slowly and stretching. Ivan wags his tail as Janet and Keegan approach. Keegan stops, focusing on his dog, then silently flashes the hand signal for 'Stay'. Ivan obediently sits as Keegan walks out the front door. Janet scoops up Minka, cradling her in her arms, then watches through the side entrance window as the taillights of both cars are swallowed up by darkness.

Feeling fidgety, Janet reconsiders Maxwell's words and returns to the bedroom, setting a sleepy Minka on Ava's satin slipper chair. She kneels in front of the cabinet. *False wall, you say?* She opens the cabinet doors, then gingerly taps on an interior wood wall with one finger. It sounds flat. She then raps on the wall with her knuckles. The wood sounds dense. Singular. She reaches deep inside the cabinet and knocks on the furthest back wall. The wood echoes back, sounding hollow – *bingo!* This must be how the letter floated through. She turns away momentarily but freezes when she hears the coarse creak and moan of aged wood repositioning itself.

Turning back, she peers inside the cabinet, then stares in disbelief as the back wall separates, then tilts forward. It is a slow-motion movement that seems carefully orchestrated – *for her?*

She leans forward into the cabinet's darkness and sees a gleaming cobalt-blue curve of something solid, *such as enamel.*

Jumping to her feet, she quickly flips on the overhead light switch and then returns to the floor. Now on her hands and knees, she reaches inside the cabinet for the loose upper edge of the wooden wall and pulls it gently toward her. A sparkle of cobalt-blue enamel glistens with intrigue from its place of seclusion. Along one edge of what appears to be a decorative jewelry box, she sees the word 'Fabergé' etched in gold.

Dare she touch it? Examine it? Or should she push the false wall firmly back into place?

She hears Ivan's deep bark resonate from the front hall foyer and immediately rises to her feet.

Ivan wags his tail as Janet opens the front door to let Keegan in.

"You won't believe what I just found!" she says breathlessly.

Keegan looks perplexed but wordlessly follows Janet back to Ava's bedroom and watches as she kneels before the nightstand.

"Well, you have to get down here with me!" Janet says, motioning to Keegan with an anxious wave.

Keegan kneels beside Janet and looks inside the cabinet. "What? I don't see anything," he says.

Janet tugs on a corner of the short wall and tilts it forward at a more pronounced angle.

"See! Here! Looks like a decorative blue enamel box with the word Fabergé, etched in gold!"

Peering into the rectangular cubby, Keegan focuses his attention and then grows momentarily silent.

"I thought you didn't want to cross that line. Didn't you say it was an invasion of your employer's privacy or something along those lines?"

Janet runs her fingers through her hair, feeling the brightness of the overhead bedroom light and Keegan's lack of understanding, somewhat irritating.

"It's not like I deliberately separated the back wall from the cabinet's interior. It fell forward on its own as I was standing beside it!"

"*Really*?!" Keegan asks with obvious disbelief. "Let's take a step back," he says calmly. "Enjoy another non-alcoholic or alcoholic drink. Or, how about that dessert you dished up earlier this evening? *Shall we?* It's been a wild night with a ghost sighting, an intruder, and now this hidden treasure."

Glancing about the room, Janet concedes that taking a step back might be a good idea, then holds out a hand for Keegan to help her to her feet. Janet leads Keegan to the kitchen, and he watches from the swivel counter stool as she dishes up berries and cubes of melon with a scoop of ice cream and a swirl of whipped cream topping.

"So, here's what I'm thinking," Janet says, handing Keegan a ceramic dessert bowl, "if Ava and Richard don't know about the Fabergé box, wouldn't we be wise helping them to discover it as Maxwell suggested?"

They eat dessert in silence, pondering their precarious situation.

"Dare we look inside the Fabergé box?" Janet finally asks with a timid smile.

"Are you able to push the false wall back into place after we have a look?"

"I think so," Janet responds.

They return to Ava's bedroom and silently kneel before the Rococo nightstand. Janet tugs the wall gently forward and reaches behind it for the enamel box, inadvertently catching sight of a brown, legal-sized envelope.

"Wow! Feels like we're uncovering artifacts from an archaeological dig!" Janet exclaims with awestruck wonderment. "And what's this, some kind of legal documentation?"

"Maybe we shouldn't..." Keegan cautions.

"Oops," Janet says with one hand, tugging the envelope loose from its hiding place. "Maybe we should decide whether we discover the mysteries of this haunted house and nightstand right now. I mean, we've seen a ghost, I've discovered a long-lost letter from Ava's mother, and now the discovery of this jewelry box. How much more other-worldly encouragement do we need?"

Their eyes meet as if in a game of truth or dare, but they say nothing. Curiosity has sparked their sense of adventure and imagination. Janet draws in a deep breath and pulls the legal-sized envelope out from behind the decorative box and then the box from their respective hiding places. The jewelry box feels weighty for its compact size. A little larger than, say, a wristlet clutch handbag. The box is glassy-smooth in her hands.

"Wow, this is really something! Look how it glows!" she says, straightening her back and holding the box eye-level. "The color! What color would you call this?"

"Blue?" Keegan answers simply.

Janet casts Keegan a sideways glance... "*Not just blue!*" she says emphatically, "but midnight ice blue with a grayish glaze."

"Hey, isn't Fabergé Russian?" Keegan asks.

"Definitely something I could research. Should I lift the lid?" she asks.

Keegan reaches out, gingerly touching the box. "It doesn't look fragile. I'm sure you won't damage anything by lifting the lid."

"It's stuck." Then with more force, Janet jiggles and lifts the lid from the Fabergé box. Keegan flinches as she emits a startled gasp. They stare in amazement at a three-strand exquisite diamond necklace centered with an oval, pink-colored diamond laid out on timeworn pink velvet.

"Unbelievable!" Janet says. "Diamonds for sure, and any idea what type of stone this center gem might be?"

"I'm guessing, a pink sapphire?" Keegan answers with eyes intently focused on the center stone.

"Wow!" Janet utters, "I'm the furthest thing from a gemologist, but even I can tell this is a magnificent piece of jewelry! *What was I thinking,* removing this valuable item from the cabinet?! I wonder if I should remove my fingerprints?!"

Janet anxiously begins rubbing the box with a corner of her shirt.

"You aren't taking anything, Janet!" Keegan exclaims, "You're just looking, then putting it back."

Janet replaces the jewelry box lid, then cautiously places the box back behind the interior wall.

She picks up and examines the legal-sized envelope. It has faded to a yellowy brown, and the edges look thin and worn. She lifts the envelope flap and sees that the glue line meant to seal the envelope has dried to a speckled gleam. She draws out several weighty sheets of cream-colored paper.

Keegan is seated next to Janet, and she angles the documents toward him so he can easily look on. The top document states that a 'Transfer on Death Deed' is a legal instrument to transfer interest in real property. The Grantor Owner, **Beverly Rose Fleming,** terminates ("quits") any right and claim to the property, thereby allowing the right or claim to transfer to the Grantee Beneficiary: **Maxwell Hemingway, III.** The property conveyed (transferred) **is a ten-acre parcel of** land on Diamond Lake, MN.

A note scribbled to Beverly Rose explains that *'The Minnesota TOD deed form allows a property to be automatically transferred to a new owner when the current owner dies, without the need to go through probate.'*

The form is notarized with an official Minnesota Secretary of State seal.

"Lucky *SOB*," Keegan says. "This is a decent gift from Ava's mother to Maxwell. Does it give a property location?"

"There is some reference to a *lakeside property*; here, you look...." Janet says.

"That's a valuable piece of real estate!" Keegan exclaims as he reviews the top document held in Janet's hands. "If I'm reading the location correctly, this property isn't far from Ava's home!"

Janet pauses to consider the evening's events before responding.

"We can't tell Maxwell about this," she says, her voice becoming low and conspiratorial. "Ava has to be the one to discover it!"

"I agree," Keegan responds.

Janet assembles the legal documents and then slides them back into the envelope with a puzzled look. She returns the brown envelope to its resting place against the far back wall of the cabinet, then re-positions the enamel jewelry box. The false division of the nightstand groans uneasily as she maneuvers it back into place.

"Funny that Maxwell didn't discover this hidden treasure earlier. It doesn't seem like it was that difficult to find."

Keegan nods in agreement.

"I want to show you one other thing I found. In the nightstand's top drawer, under Maxwell's letter." Janet rises to her knees, pulling the nightstand's top drawer halfway out. She retrieves the gray envelope and returns to the floor, where the carpet offers softened comfort. The pages are letter-folded, creating three panels on each side of the paper. Janet shows Keegan the ragged-edged pages as she unfolds them, "It's as though the pages were torn from a journal then thoughtfully folded," she says, "and there were dried rose petals pressed inside the envelope," she adds, motioning to the top of the nightstand where the pale rose-colored petals lay scattered.

She waves the pages gently under her nose. The papers have retained a faintly floral essence. She sneaks a glimpse at Keegan for his response but cannot read his expression as he sits in silence beside her.

The handwriting is smooth with rounded letters, as though written with great care by someone with a feminine flair for penmanship. The ivory-colored papers have a thick linen texture which may have prevented the ink from feathering or fading.

"Well," she says with mild surprise, "there are only two sentences on this first page."

'Believing doesn't depend on knowing, only trusting that there's more.
There's always more.'

"What a curious entry," Janet says. Then, hesitantly, she adds, "Maybe I shouldn't..."

"I think it would be okay to read," Keegan responds. "Ava's mother most likely wrote it, and she's passed on. No secrets now. Too late for that."

Janet nods decisively, then takes a moment to compose herself before reading the following several pages.

"Life, I realize, is a mystical experience and never what we think. The arc of one's life is a necessary balm

for our wounds. In the second half of life, you try to understand what happened in the first half. The older you are, the more you know certain things. The longer you've lived, the more urgency you feel about making things right before you go.

I've had my share of indiscretions and regrets and lived with the consequences. I should have been by my daughter's side during her recovery from a brain injury. I traveled often and unnecessarily because it was the way of the jet setters. I was a Hollywood starlet, distracted by the fame and drama of my success. Now that Ava's nanny and many of our staff have passed or moved on, I think of the people who loved and supported our little family of three. Faithful friends and the household staff - all mattered.

Janet looks at Keegan, who is still staring straight ahead, fully concentrating on something, it seems, beyond the words Janet is reading. She continues...

The Hemingways were particularly supportive when Sebastian and I briefly separated. The Hemingways became the family I never knew. Sebastian's affair with Mona, the only affair I could not ignore, is now too difficult and painful to write about. The necklace that Mona later wore, an identical replica from our movie 'Forever', as if to mock me. I recall the thoughtful visits and support from the Hemingways. My dear friend and trusted confidant, Phyllis Hemingway, will forever be in my heart. Although young, Maxwell Hemingway was a reliable friend to Ava and me. I appreciated his optimism and enthusiasm for life. The Hemingway's presence in our lives truly mattered."

"That's it," Janet says. "This is where the letter or journal entry ends except for the initials **BRF**."

Janet holds the papers carefully in both hands, turning each page over as if looking for more clues on the empty back pages.

"Ava's mother seems to have valued the Hemingway's friendship, but she misunderstood Maxwell. I would hardly call Maxwell an exemplary friend."

"Maybe there were qualities Beverly Rose saw in Maxwell that he has since abandoned," Keegan says, "or we just don't see. What is it she wrote...?

Believing doesn't depend on knowing, only trusting that there's more. There's always more."

Janet looks in disbelief at Keegan, surprised that he doesn't see the truth about his friend, Maxwell. "Maxwell *is 'more'* all right, 'more' self-absorbed, and 'more' of an opportunist than you care to admit."

Keegan looks away, remembering the past. "Maxwell was an okay guy growing up and quite a golfer with a great backswing. It was exciting to watch him play."

"Are you saying Maxwell's years of success and quiet 'golf' applause changed him?" Janet asks.

Keegan gives a hesitant nod as Janet looks down at the ivory pages still in her grasp.

"Ava needs to read this," she says with quiet conviction.

"And Maxwell deserves to know," Keegan adds.

CHAPTER ELEVEN

A WEDDING NECKLACE

Before opening her eyes, Janet feels the satisfying warmth of Keegan lying beside her. She remembers last night: Keegan's tender embrace and the tumble they took laughing as they fell across the soft downy loft of bedding. It was Ivan jumping effortlessly from floor to bed that caused them to roll to the middle of the bed and a little off-center. Minka, unable to make the jump, whimpered from the floor.

"Ivan, down," Keegan ordered.

With a heavy bounce, the German shepherd jumped from bed to floor. Minka, then satisfied, curled into her fleecy circular bed beside them. With Ivan lying beside Minka, the two settled in for an all-night slumber.

It wasn't at all what Janet expected for their first overnight. They never pulled back the sateen duvet to experience the subtle extravagance of Egyptian cotton percale sheets against their naked bodies and make passionate love. Instead, they cuddled, pretty much fully clothed, satisfied to rest on the down-filled bedding with lavender-scented pillows.

At first, Janet found herself distracted by the dogs' presence and heavy breathing, then the house security system - *had she set the alarm?* Then, Ava's treasure trove hidden behind a false wall of the Rococo nightstand. Her mind finally settled on the sensation of Keegan's fingertips lightly stroking her forearm. There was, at last, an overwhelming sense of relaxation, of letting go of all concern in those quiet moments of darkness. There was pillow talk, of course. But it was more conversational than romantic. Keegan asking Janet about life on the East Coast. Janet was hesitant at first but understood Keegan's silence as interest until she realized he was quiet. Too quiet. Sound asleep quiet.

"You have awakened something in me that feels right," she whispered into the darkness above Keegan. "I don't want to rush this relationship, but I feel our spirits connecting."

She looked at his handsome face, sure he had not heard her.

Now, with morning light streaming into the bedroom, Janet watches Keegan slowly awaken. She had been awake for some time, lying in the room's stillness and wondering if Keegan's feelings for her were complicated by his friendship with Maxwell and his inheritance from the late Beverly Rose Fleming or the more obvious issue of Ava's haunted mansion.

Keegan rolls on his side, facing Janet, and kisses her tenderly. "I begin my mornings with a shower," he says. "How about it? Care to join me?"

The idea of taking it slowly last night quickly becomes an irresistible urge to touch and feel Keegan in the most intimate way. Natural, sensual, fantastic. Nothing rational about the impulses or desires stirring within her now.

She dreamily recalls an ad she saw in a travel magazine for *White Sands* adults-only resorts picturing a blissfully serene couple standing waist-deep at the edge of an infinity pool (designer cocktails in hand) with a mesmerizing panoramic view of the Caribbean Ocean and cerulean blue sky above and beyond.

'The clearest waters anyone has ever seen,' the caption read. The ad invites readers 'to be as free as the sea.'

The scenery and couple a bit too perfect, but the ad is enticingly beautiful with its allure of a fantasy vacation designed for two.

How long had it been? *Years too long.*

Did she want to be as free as the sea? *Well, not necessarily.* But the thought of a new beginning quickens her heart. Her instincts take over as she begins to undress. Then, feeling Keegan's eyes upon her, she looks back with a sultry smile before walking toward the spacious en suite bathroom.

"I've got to let the dogs out," Keegan says, looking back as the dogs begin to whine. "Hold that thought," he says with a wink. "I'll be there in a moment."

She stands contemplating, then completely undresses, wrapping herself in a fluffy white bath sheet. Janet reaches into the shower, opening the faucets to an oversized square rain shower head of warming spray. The shower looks too inviting to wait. She drops her towel and steps into the shower to experience a waterfall of full-body soak. As soothing and natural as standing in a tropical island rainfall. The water flows through her thick tangle of dark hair, then sensually down her back—an experience she imagines as luxurious as anything *White Sands* adults-only resorts might offer.

Through the glistening spray, she turns to see Keegan's bronzed, athletic body on the other side of the misting glass shower door and remembers her first visit to Diamond Lake just weeks earlier. She recalls the neighboring man-sized Grecian lawn statue of a virile-winged Cupid, poised with bow and arrow, knee-deep in tufted prairie grass.

At the time, she wondered which sequestered home this naked messenger of love might belong to. Now she knew - *he belonged to her.*

◆ ◆ ◆

It's midday Sunday afternoon when Keegan and Janet part ways. Keegan has 'stuff to do' on his property and dog food and groceries to buy. They end their weekend at the halfway point of the Caribou coffee shop with a cappuccino for Janet and a Café Americano for Keegan.

"So, will you be okay alone tonight?" Keegan asks. The aroma of brewing coffee fills the café with a familiar roasted fragrance and faint notes of chocolate which Janet gratefully inhales.

"I'll be okay by myself tonight. I have Minka to protect me," she smiles over the noisy hum of grinding coffee beans. "Tomorrow is a workday, and who knows when the workers will arrive? I don't think anyone wants to be surprised, me or the housekeepers."

She lifts her head, looking out the window at the

bustling Caribou parking lot, anticipating Keegan's absence and the emptiness it will bring to this Sunday afternoon. She knows how silly she is being. After all, she is a forty-seven-year-old woman experienced in romance and the uncertainties of life. What she *has* discovered is that Keegan is a passionate lover. Just thinking of their morning hours of lovemaking from the shower to bed and shower again causes her to blush. The desire and satisfaction she felt more than once causes warmth to pulsate through her body, even now. She doesn't want this day with Keegan to end.

Keegan holds his coffee cup steady, with a moment of hesitation before asking, "Are you really okay with everything that's happened this weekend?"

Janet wonders if Keegan heard her whisper last night when she believed him to be asleep. "I thought I needed more time," she says with some hesitation.

"So... how do you feel now?" he asks.

Feeling her face grow warm, Janet answers with a playful grin, "I've already decided where I will have your name tattooed on my body. Does that answer your question?"

Keegan laughs, pulling his chair closer to Janet, as he reaches for her hand under the café table. Janet then wonders if *Keegan* needed more time before taking their relationship to the next level. It had been a kind of whirlwind romance. *Too much? Too soon?* She wonders.

Was he still recovering from his first marriage so long ago? Or was another woman in the picture? It was a possibility. If she'd learned anything this past weekend, it was to believe, as Beverly Rose put it, 'that there's more (to the story). There's always more'.

Janet and Keegan part ways with a kiss. Janet watches Keegan drive away with his German shepherd in the passenger seat. She can't help but sigh and fall into a bit of fantasy, imagining herself returning to Keegan's house, then helping him in his garden, watering plants and flowers as Ivan roams the yard, then trails behind with companionable interest.

Later the two of them lazily cooking an Italian dinner – something with spicy meatballs - and jazzy Dave Brubeck piano music with amplified volume, as though the famed musician were right there in the room playing just for them.

Janet returns to Ava's house, parking her Honda in the wide-open lot. Everything about the place now feels oversized and empty. She is grateful when Minka greets her at the door with a wag of her tail. She tidies up her guest bedroom, packing clothing items into her overnight bag. In Ava's bedroom, she brushes the strewn rose petals into the upper drawer of the heirloom nightstand. She opens the lower compartment to be sure nothing is out of the ordinary.

It's another mild autumn day. Janet takes Minka for a stroll along the sandy path, skirting a rocky portion of shoreline that looks out at a sun-splashed Diamond Lake. Her best ideas always come to her while she is walking.

She needs clarity. Her mind wanders to Keegan. Had she laid too much on him with the mystery surrounding the necklace and Maxwell? And what about the jeweled necklace? Why has it remained mysteriously hidden for so many years, even since Ava's parents passed away? And how will she encourage Ava to investigate beyond the letters she and Elaine have discovered?

Her mind wanders to Ava's childhood bedtime story of a young lady (a 'princess,' of course) and her royal family that fled their 'kingdom' for safety reasons. The family left the extravagant lifestyle they had known only to arrive in another land and struggle for survival.

"The important thing," Ava had said, "is that mother and daughter stayed together."

She knows her idea is far-fetched, but thinking about the Fabergé jewelry box, she wonders whether Beverly Rose had ties with the Imperial Romanov family.

Didn't the Tsar of Russia commission the jeweled Fabergé Easter eggs for his wife and mother?

Was Beverly Rose then perhaps a descendant of Russian royalty?

Janet had heard of people who believed themselves to be descendants of the Romanovs. *But was it true?* Is it possible that a great-grandmother or grandfather was somehow able to escape the years of bloody civil war with some of the royal jewels?

Janet had studied Russian Literature at the University of MN and recalls stories of Tsar Nicholas, Tsarina Alexandra, their children, and their untimely and horrific deaths.

Did Sebastian's or Beverly Rose's family escape the Russian Revolution? Her mind automatically lands on Sebastian as the Russian who has the remarkably resilient look of a survivor, even though he may have just been a relative to those fleeing Russia. On the other hand, Beverly Rose has a royal's solemn beauty and stately appearance.

Janet's mind wanders again to the cobalt blue box inscription-Fabergé. Were Sebastian or Beverly Rose somehow involved with the Fabergé family?

Janet returns to the house with Minka, then downstairs to her office, and logs on to her desktop computer.

She types **Fabergé** into the search engine QUERRY, then scrolls down, reading:

'House of Fabergé'

The Bolsheviks seized the House of Fabergé in 1918.

'The Romanovs owned many of the Fabergé collections... Then, during the Russian revolution, the Bolsheviks ransacked the palaces and stores, and thousands of pieces of Fabergé disappeared, eventually to be discovered in jewelry collections scattered throughout the world.'

Janet scrolls through the online information and discovers that Peter Carl Fabergé and his family fled Russia to various parts of Europe.

And another story recounts royal family members who fled Russia in 1917 on a warship sent by the royal's cousin, Britain's King George V.

The historical stories no doubt paralleled the bedtime story Ava's mother told. *But why hide jewels in the nightstand?*

Out of curiosity, Janet types 'found property' into the search engine. It basically states that if the found property is lost or abandoned, the person who discovers it gets to keep it.

So, what were the Flemings afraid of?

The Russian government insisting their jewels be returned to them? To place the necklace in one of Moscow's Museums seemed a ridiculously far-fetched idea.

Feeling suddenly ravenous, Janet remembers

Keegan's left-over restaurant appetizers from Saturday night and heads upstairs with Minka at her heels. *Overnight.* Last night and this morning now feel like some far-off marvelous memory.

Still sipping what is left of her lukewarm coffee, she settles into a swivel kitchen stool beside the counter to enjoy her impromptu meal of cold chicken wings. Unable to resist grabbing a chicken wing directly from the container, she bites into it with great satisfaction. The wings have been marinating overnight in rich barbeque sauce, and the flavor fills her mouth with a tangy sweetness. But before she can take another delicious bite, the kitchen phone rings. "Ava Fleming residence," she answers, still chewing.

"Hi, Janet. Elaine here. I just spoke with Richard and change of plans. Ava and Richard *are returning home* midday on Monday."

Janet suddenly sits up straight. Her eyes dart around the kitchen, noticing a small stack of dirty dishes near the sink.

She makes a quick mental note: *Must tidy up kitchen!*

"How's everything going at the house?" Elaine asks.

Janet rolls her eyes. *Where to begin?*

After a thoughtful pause, Janet responds, "Well, I do have some interesting developments that contain elements of the otherworldly."

"Care to elaborate?"

"It has to do with this spirited home and hidden treasure. How's that for intrigue?" Janet smiles.

"Say no more," Elaine answers. "I'll be right over."

When Elaine appears, entering through the kitchen door, Janet feels an immediate sense of relief. Elaine, never one to dress casually, is wearing black dress trousers and a cream cashmere sweater with diamond stud earrings.

Elaine, always perfectly proper and ladylike, Janet smiles to herself.

She welcomes Elaine's polite, even-tempered energy and the opportunity to share confidences with her co-worker. Finally, there is a chance that they might untangle this series of mysteries together.

Janet offers Elaine a generous pour from the remaining bottle of Sauvignon Blanc and pours another glass for herself as she reasons they might as well finish off the bottle. Somehow having the long-stemmed wine glass in hand steadies her.

"I would like to begin by saying that what I discovered this weekend was '*revealed*' to me. I didn't go snooping for anything. Honest," she says, looking straight at Elaine and holding up her right hand as if swearing on a stack of Bibles.

"Bring your wine; you'll need it for this moment of revelation."

Janet leads Elaine to Ava's bedroom.

"We'll need the overhead light on," she says, reaching for the wall switch.

Janet sets her wine glass on the nightstand and then kneels on the carpet. She reaches deep to loosen and tug at the interior back wall of the Rococo nightstand.

Elaine stands very still. Quietly watching as Janet draws the oblong-shaped blue enamel box from the lower cupboard, then presents it at an angle to display the words Fabergé etched in gold.

"To be clear, I investigated because I heard the slow

groan of wood as I stood in the very spot you are now standing. As you once told me, *you've* had supernatural experiences in this home when working alone..."

Elaine shifts her standing position from one foot to the other, looking curiously at Janet.

"What exactly did you find there?" Elaine asks.

"Well, full disclosure, there have been ghost sightings this weekend, and Maxwell has been hanging around. Thankfully, a well-behaved Keegan was here to run interference for me. Keegan was here by invitation. Maxwell was not."

Janet glances around the room cautiously, holding the Fabergé box steady for Elaine to see.

"Maxwell is intent on finding a treasure trove hidden within this nightstand. According to Maxwell, Ava has been confiding in Cassandra, saying that her mother told bedtime stories of a princess and hidden treasure in a well-loved piece of furniture and family that fled their homeland. So, I thought, Russian? The Russian Revolution? Has the story been exaggerated over time, or is there truth to it?"

"So, you think Ava is a descendant of the Russian royal family?" Elaine asks with a hint of sputter.

"Well, I didn't exactly say 'royal.' I did some research today and typed in 'House of Fabergé'. I read that there were thousands of Fabergé pieces, most now scattered across faraway lands, so I guess it could have been a non-royal."

Elaine sits down on Ava's bed with a puzzled look.

"It's estimated that as many as two million Russians left or were expelled from Russia during the 1920s and 1930s." Janet continues, "I typed in 'Found Property,' and guess what? *The person who found the property gets to keep it unless the original owner claims it,* so the rule is finders keepers."

"How would this 'found property' of a blue Fabergé jewelry box help Ava, who already has a collection of jewels and pricey artwork?" Elaine asks.

"Great question, but I'm thinking more about mystery and mysticism. So much of life is bewildering. We will never know it all. Consider what you and I have experienced, with no obvious explanation. This discovery may open a spiritual portal to Ava's mother and father. She has her high society lake friends but no family to speak of. *Where are they? Who are they?*"

"Also, I did not say the box was *empty,*" Janet adds after a microsecond's pause.

Shaking out her hands, Elaine says, "Okay, enough suspense! Let's open the Fabergé box already!"

Janet lifts the jewelry box cover, presenting the three-strand diamond necklace with its extraordinary pink star focal point to Elaine.

"*Magnificent!*" Elaine gasps. "So, this is what bedazzled the tsars?" Then after a moment of quiet reflection, she asks, "But why keep this fabulous piece of jewelry hidden?"

Thoroughly intrigued, Elaine turns to lean directly over Janet and the box, "Is there more to the jewelry box? A false bottom or tray beneath the necklace, perhaps?"

"I'm so glad you're here! You are brilliant!" Janet says with a sly smile.

Janet cautiously removes the velvet tray and necklace, setting the items on the bed beside Elaine. Tucked within the box, she discovers the picture of a woman wearing a diamond tiara neatly folded in thirds. The words **Duchess Zara yr. 1915**, appears written in long hand through a crease in the vintage photo.

"Is Beverly Rose Duchess Zara?" Janet asks with a look of astonishment. "They certainly resemble each other!"

Elaine and Janet make sudden eye contact, "Let's QUERRY her!" they say in unison.

Janet hands the sepia photo of Duchess Zara to Elaine, trading it for the cover of the jewelry box, then gathers the weighty necklace and places it back inside the Fabergé box. She returns the box and necklace to the nightstand. The two women hurry downstairs to Janet's computer.

On a hunch, Janet types in 'Duchess Zara, Russia,' and a blurb of history pops up in the search engine.

Duchess Zara Romanov, Russia --

'Born at the turn of the century, Duchess Zara Romanov left Russia with her family between 1917 - 1918. Duchess Zara was one of about a dozen Russian Romanov relatives who escaped the Bolsheviks and the Russian Revolution of 1917.

Duchess Zara Romanov, it was noted, 'never married.' She lived out her later years in California working as a landscape artist, deliberately avoiding media attention.'

Elaine shakes her head, "The dates don't match up. Ava's mother, Beverly Rose, was born in 1921. She was born *after* the start of the Russian Revolution."

"So, is Duchess Zara *the mother* of Beverly Rose Fleming? Their likeness is remarkable. Was Beverly Rose perhaps an illegitimate daughter?" Janet asks.

"Possible scenario," Janet adds, "could be that there was shame over Beverly Rose being illegitimate? In addition, guilt or dishonor for leaving Russia and their ill-fated relatives behind?"

"Oh, look at this," Janet says as she scrolls through the QUERRY page, "a picture of Duchess Zara's necklace, perhaps?

It says, 'Other notable jewelry the royals wore included lavish designs with rubies, emeralds, sapphires, and diamonds. Most works were commissioned by the imperial family, particularly for weddings.'

Was *this* a wedding necklace, then? And what became of the fiancé? Duchess Zara's wedding necklace, maybe, and no wedding?"

"Yes, this makes sense," Elaine says. "When Beverly Rose met Sebastian, he reinvented her, making up a fake backstory to hide the shame of her illegitimacy and Russian royal heritage."

Elaine holds out her hands, 'weighing' them in the air, "I've read that in the early days of Hollywood, studios would go to great lengths to market certain images to audiences. Was Beverly Rose advised or forced to hide her mother's and family's identity? Was it some deep, dark secret? Makes you wonder what else Beverly Rose was forced to hide?"

"How sad," Janet interjects. "No wonder her spirit is restless."

Janet suddenly grasps the edge of her desk with both hands, "*What was that?*" she asks Elaine with a startled flinch.

"What? Nothing. I don't see anything," Elaine answers with a quick turn of her head, her eyes searching the room behind and around them.

They hear a dull boom, a noise that seems to emanate

from deep within the house. They instinctively draw back from the computer, listening intently, then glance at one another for reassurance.

"I could have sworn I saw someone standing over there," Janet says, pointing to a far corner of the room near her office doorway. She feels a tingling sensation move through her entire body.

Elaine crosses the room to the doorway and looks down the long hallway past her own office, "Nothing there," she reports back to Janet.

"Did you at least hear that booming sound?" Janet asks.

"Well...yes, but this is a big house with lots of interesting mechanical noises," Elaine carefully responds as if trying to convince herself.

"You're right. Probably a water pipe," Janet says, taking a moment to collect her thoughts. Then adds halfheartedly, "Is that really what a water pipe sounds like? Oh, what do I know? I live in an apartment..."

She sighs and drops her arms to her sides, then looks out the window, resting her eyes on a dense cluster of autumn-colored trees. Late afternoon was giving way to a pale sigh of deepening blue sky.

"So, let's say Beverly Rose meets stage actor Sebastian Fleming, who outranks her in age and experience, and he reinvents her for Hollywood. Is this what we are thinking?"

"And..." Elaine adds, "Are we to assume that the necklace is one of the thousands of pieces of Fabergé jewelry plundered from the palaces of the Romanovs - or – is this the property, the wedding necklace of Duchess Zara Romanov, a Russian émigré? Are Beverly Rose and, thereby, Ava descendants of the Royal Romanov family?"

"Now what?" Janet asks in a small, uncertain voice. "Do we show Ava the presumed wedding necklace and photo of her grandmother, Duchess Zara? Do we offer Ava our hypothetical explanation or simply wait for fate to take its course?"

Elaine takes a step toward the window. "It suddenly occurs to me," she says with a steady wondrous gaze, "that life is more about *whose* fate we follow. Fate, then, must bring this family together."

Although still trying to understand *how* or *why*, Janet nods in agreement.

CHAPTER TWELVE

SIMPLICITY IS CHARMING

Sunday night

"Miss me?" Keegan asks teasingly when he answers Janet's call.

"More than you know," Janet answers with a laugh. She props two pillows under her head, then stares past the foot of the bed.

"How was your afternoon?" she asks in a light-hearted voice.

"Pretty great. Living the life of a rugged woodsman, raking leaves, saving them for compost, then trimming back a few trees. You might as well know you're in a relationship with a bona fide tree hugger. And you? Any more discoveries found in that mystical mansion you are guarding?"

In a relationship? Seriously. Did she hear Keegan correctly? Did he just say they were 'in a relationship'?

"Oh gosh," Janet replies after a moment's hesitation to regain her composure.

"Elaine and I found a picture of someone wearing a tiara that we believe to be Ava's grandmother. It was tucked inside that blue Fabergé jewelry box. *Duchess Zara yr. 1915* was handwritten across the photo, so we researched the name and found a small bio but no picture online. Duchess Zara emigrated with her family from Russia around the time of the Russian Revolution. Then lived out her later years somewhat reclusively in Southern California, working as an artist."

"Did Ava know her grandmother?" Keegan asks.

"During the eight years she's been employed by the Fleming Family Foundation, Elaine never heard Ava mention an immediate *or* extended family, so our guess is '*no.*' We believe Ava knows nothing of her Russian heritage. Exciting news though: we believe the grandmother is descended from the royal Romanov family."

"Not completely surprising, I guess. My aunt Sheila Livingston has some sort of distinguished royal British title. She has dual citizenship in both the UK and the US." Keegan pauses before continuing, "Dozens of people have claimed to be descendants of the royal Romanov family. You know – *wannabes*. Mostly imposters," he adds.

Janet takes a long breath before speaking again. Keegan's lack of astonishment surprises her, especially given the horrific outcome of the Romanov dynasty. "I don't think she's an imposter or a wannabe," she says while rearranging her pillow for more head support. "This entire reveal would most likely astonish Ava. So, here's the million-dollar question. How do we inform Ava of her possible royal heritage and her mother's letters and documents?"

Keegan says nothing, so Janet continues...

"Maybe let Ava somehow 'appear' to discover the treasure and documents herself? Maybe I hear the groan of wood inside the nightstand, for instance, then curiously look inside, and suddenly all is revealed with me standing by to assist?"

"Hmm. Impressive plan, but how would you just be *standing by*'? And more importantly, how would you time the false wall to fall forward?"

"Call it a coincidence," Janet replies. "I retrieve the letter from her mother to Maxwell, which she already knows is in the top drawer of the Rococo nightstand, and then present that second letter and suddenly *'fake hear'* the mysterious groan of wood ungluing itself from the lower level of the cabinet. I kneel to investigate, and *Eureka!* Look what *we've* discovered!"

"You're quite imaginative!" Keegan says with a laugh. "Ever thought of writing a mystery novel, Agatha Christie?"

Janet smiles at the compliment.

"But seriously," Keegan adds, "Having Ava beside you is a good idea. That will give her a sense of self-discovery."

◆ ◆ ◆

On Monday morning, Janet awakens to the chatter of housekeepers outside her bedroom door. Sarah opens the guest bedroom door and pokes her head into the room. "Oh, forgot you were in here!" the housekeeper says with a look of mock surprise.

Janet knows it's a ruse to see what she's up to and perhaps the condition of the guest bedroom she's been occupying these past few days. She glances at her side table alarm clock. 5:00 am. Ugh. She decides to snuggle deep into her sumptuous bedding and go back to sleep, but just as Janet snuggles under the comforter, Sarah powers up the vacuum cleaner. She gives it several noisy bangs against the closed door. Resigned to the inevitable commotion that will most certainly follow, Janet rolls out of bed and stumbles wearily into the shower.

◆ ◆ ◆

Ava and Richard return home earlier than expected with a dizzying amount of fuss. The limo driver approaches the house, stopping at the grand entrance portico. The driver jumps out to open the car door, and the couple emerges from the limo, with Ava sounding like a whiny adolescent.

"I told you I need my cosmetic case *NOW*, Richard. Tell the driver I must have my Gucci overnight bag."

"Ava, the luggage is tightly packed into the car's trunk. I'm sure the driver will unload the luggage as quickly as possible through the garage/kitchen entrance."

Ava glares at Richard over the top of her shiny transparent pink sunglasses. The driver pulls forward, through the circular drive to the side door entrance, unloads the luggage, and then rolls it through the garage and into the kitchen.

The housekeepers have left for the day, but Fiona is in the kitchen prepping for dinner. With Fiona's assistance, Janet receives the luggage arranging it into groupings of what belongs to whom. She overhears Ava loudly reprimanding Richard from the front hall foyer, then calling out her name. Janet hoists Ava's Gucci overnight bag over one shoulder, then grabs a piece of oversized luggage in each hand. The luggage whirs and clacks, echoing through the hallway as Janet rolls it along the marble floors, then into Ava's bedroom, where her employer is already undressing, throwing outer garments across the bed.

Ava barely looks up when Janet enters the room. "Where are my casual clothes?" Ava orders more than asks of her assistant.

Janet abandons the rolling luggage in her grasp, sets the overnight bag on a side chair, then disappears into Ava's closet. She reappears with a lightweight oversized jersey top and matching coral-colored joggers. "I'll unpack your suitcases and set aside clothing for the laundry," Janet offers.

"Yes, yes, that will be fine, but first, bring me the letter my mother wrote to Maxwell. Some things were brought to my attention in Beverly Hills over the weekend. It seems, for instance, that I have a grandmother I never met or knew of", she says simply.

Janet feels a flush of adrenaline tingle through her body as she reimagines how to introduce Ava to the treasured items and documents hidden within the antique nightstand. The discovery now seems a more urgent matter.

"There are actually two letters for you," Janet says, slowly drawing the letters from the drawer. "One of the letters caught and crumpled on the underside of the drawer as I was trying to close it the other day. Elaine and I believe there may be another compartment in the lower half of the nightstand."

Ava gives Janet a sudden, startled look. "How do you know about that?" she asks with a wavering of mistrust and suspicion.

"Well, well, I don't really," Janet lies, taking a step back. "It's just an observation, as the second letter seems to have appeared from nowhere."

"I'll take *both* letters," Ava announces with an air of authority, extending her arm. "Richard and I will read the letters this evening - *together*."

"Certainly," Janet responds as she hands both letters over to her employer.

Ava gives Janet a dismissive wave, and Janet leaves the room before unpacking Ava's luggage.

An hour later, Ava calls Janet through the house intercom. "Janet, please come up." The phone clicks off.

Janet looks blankly at the wall, then takes a deep calming breath. Finally, she walks slowly up the stairs to Ava's bedroom, contemplating her predicament.

"You called for me?" she asks Ava meekly from across the room.

"Yes," Ava answers. "What does this second letter mean, and why are the pages so raggedy?"

"Are you asking me to review the second letter for you?" Janet responds, somewhat confused by this turn of events.

Ava is standing near the Rococo nightstand. "Well, of course. I wish you to make some sense of it".

Janet steps forward to accept the ivory-colored pages from her employer while striving for a helpful, optimistic attitude. She silently re-reads the journal entries sensing Ava's steady gaze upon her.

"Well, as I see it, your mother is reflecting upon her life and wishes to thank the people who supported and helped her during a brief, or possibly an extended time of emotional need," Janet says warily. "My guess is that the pages are 'ragged' because they were torn directly from a diary or journal."

"And what is this nonsense about the Hemingways?" Ava asks, her face reddening with irritation.

"Apparently," Janet says, "your mother believed the Hemingways were wonderful, loyal friends. Also, something about a necklace from the movie '*Forever*' that broke your mother's heart...sorry to say."

"You needn't mention this to Richard. I will tell him in my own time," Ava says, purposely avoiding eye contact with her assistant.

"Ah, of course. As you wish," Janet replies. "Would you be interested in discovering where the second letter came from?"

"Not at this time," Ava answers in a softer tone. "By the way, be on the lookout for some artwork arriving special delivery. The grandmother I never knew, it seems, was an artist, of all things. An art gallery owner contacted me while Richard and I were in California. They are shipping my grandmother's artwork to the house this week."

Janet presses one hand against her chest, "That's wonderful," she says. "I mean, how wonderful for *you*."

"Mostly wonderful for the art gallery owner who received my advance payment for who-knows-what kitschy artwork is expected to arrive," Ava snaps back.

"Well, you must have some sort of feeling regarding the discovery of a long-lost grandmother," Janet says, overwhelmed by this new information and undecided as to whether this conversation with Ava would end well.

"How about disappointment?" Ava responds with a short laugh of disbelief. "Would a phone call or birthday greeting from my only living grandmother have been too much to ask for? And where on earth am I to store this so-called artwork?" Ava asks with a dramatic sweeping gesture, then stares at her hands as if they might hold the answer.

"Well, that's all for now. Find out if Fiona has dinner ready, will you please?"

"Of course," Janet answers with a courteous nod.

She leaves Ava's bedroom, convinced that Ava's reaction to her ancestral discovery is a combination of anger and frustration. A manifestation of pain, realizing her family identity has been hidden from her all these years.

◆ ◆ ◆

When the artwork arrives late Wednesday afternoon, Ava insists that the pieces be immediately unpacked.

Raul, the groundskeeper, happens to be available for the task. He carefully removes each painting from its double-wall corrugated box, then removes the bubble wrap under Ava's watchful eye.

Ava stands at arm's length, constantly redirecting her attention and waving her hands to indicate where along an empty expanse of living room floor and wall Raul is to prop and lean the artwork whose composition is original, contemporary, and colorful. Finally, the groundskeeper gathers the cardboard and bubble wrap into a massive bundle of recycling material and clears the room of refuse.

Minka follows Ava's steady stroll as she views the artwork. But the piece that causes both Minka and Ava to stop and turn mid-step is the larger-than-life oil portrait in a heavy gold antique frame. It is the type of portrait one would hang above a fireplace with an oversized handcrafted mantel. It is a portrait, both formal and elegant, of solemn beauty. It is the portrait of an aristocratic woman wearing an elaborate bejeweled headdress and a three-strand diamond necklace with a pink star focal point.

Ava stands motionless, facing the painting, then scoops the miniature poodle into her arms. Though several feet back, Janet instantly notices the physical similarities between Ava and her grandmother.

Does Ava see the resemblance as well? Janet wonders.

There is a moment of awkward tension as the two usually chatty housekeepers and Fiona look on from a distant doorway between the kitchen and living room in hushed amazement.

Ava steps forward, moving closer to the painting of her grandmother, then reaches with her free arm to gently touch the portrait. The image is so vibrant that it seems as though the brushstrokes themselves are pulsing with life. "*I know her,*" Ava says in a faraway voice. "This woman...I know her. *We've met.*"

The only two missing from the room during this epic moment of discovery are Elaine and Mindy. Janet backs discreetly out of the living room and heads downstairs. When she arrives at their office doorway, she steps inside and, in a half-whispered voice, says, "You must see this portrait of Ava's grandmother, just delivered to the house!

The resemblance to Ava and her mother, Beverly Rose, is remarkable."

With mounting anticipation, the three office workers bound up the stairs. Janet stops mid-step suddenly, "Let's not let our excitement be too obvious," she cautions with a glance back at Mindy and Elaine, "it might make Ava anxious." The two women nod in agreement. But by the time they reach the living room, both Ava and Minka have left the room.

"Where's Ava?" Janet mouths silently to Fiona from across the room.

"What?" Fiona asks loudly, without understanding the need for discretion.

"Where's Ava?" Janet asks again, this time in a subdued, audible voice.

"In her bedroom, I guess," Fiona says with a simple shoulder shrug as she turns back toward the kitchen.

Janet, Elaine, and Mindy stand at a respectful distance from the lineup of leaning artwork, their eyes jumping from one picture to the next. The paintings are of nature, such as a field of blooming Lupine with blue-lavender flowers and soft brushstrokes of grey-green leaves. This painting has a handwritten note scrawled below the artist's signature, "*along the Russian Ridge Open Space Preserve (CA),*" and another painting of a sandpiper running along the ocean beach, leaving its tiny footprints in the sand. The works have been executed with ease and simplicity, balanced and serene with a modern art flare. Easy on the eye with large expanses of color. Janet enjoys and appreciates the singular beauty of each piece, the bright and airy themes with a whimsical tone.

The women gather before the portrait of Ava's grandmother, which stands out significantly from the others with its richly dark and dramatic colors in oil and the heavily ornate, vintage gold frame. They glance curiously at one another and then focus on the portrait.

"This piece might be a self-portrait or, because of its contrast to the other artwork, painted by another artist," Elaine suggests.

Elaine and Janet share a look. They recognize it as the same woman from the photograph they discovered tucked inside the blue Fabergé jewelry box.

Janet leans in confidentially to her co-workers and whispers, "I overheard Ava say that she *knows this woman*. Ava then stepped in closer to the painting and gently touched it."

The three women stand together, quietly contemplating the portrait and considering Ava's response. Elaine tilts her head to one side, eyebrows raised but says nothing. Mindy bends to one knee, then squats before the painting to get closer to the image of Ava's grandmother.

"Such a stunning headdress and exquisite necklace!" Mindy says. "Does anyone know if this is a Tiara and if the stones are real sapphires? If so, they are the largest sapphires I've ever seen! And the way this headdress crests reminds me of an ocean wave."

Janet acknowledges Mindy's observation with a slight nod. She then observes that the Tiara in this portrait is at least twice the size of the one in the photograph tucked within the Fabergé jewelry box. This Tiara is more of a bejeweled crown paired with the opulent three-strand diamond necklace.

"Speaking hypothetically, is this an ornamental head-dress or a Tiara?" Mindy asks. "Wouldn't a Tiara imply that she's a 'royal'? Could these be, say, crown jewels?"

Elaine and Janet exchange a knowing look behind Mindy's back.

"We'll see…" Janet says. "One thing we've learned today is that Ava recognizes the woman in the painting."

The three women return to their respective lower-level office suites, and Janet leaves for the day at five p.m. without hearing another word from Ava.

♦ ♦ ♦

She swings by Keegan's lakeside home and finds him relaxing on a cushy chaise lounge with a book in hand. Ivan sprawled lazily next to Keegan, stands to stretch, wagging his tail when he sees Janet approaching.

This sweet interlude with Keegan is as appealing as the sun's warmth upon her back. She feels the muscles in her neck and shoulders relax as she inhales the toasty fragrance of autumn in the air. Singular orange and yellow maple leaves separated from tree branches flutter to the ground, some caught in a swirl of fresh wind, blowing off the lake.

"Hola, Keegan!" she calls out, brushing soft windswept strands of hair from her face as she climbs the short stack of steps to his deck. She leans over gently to stroke Ivan's back.

Keegan looks up, squinting in the sunlight to smile at Janet with a look of yearning in his eyes. "Do I at least get a kiss?"

"Why, of course," she says, leaning over him for a smooch. He reaches up to embrace her but pulls her close, and she loses her balance, tumbling on top of him. They kiss as she snuggles in narrowly beside his muscular firmness on the cushioned chaise lounge.

"Whatcha reading?" she asks.

"A book about the Golden Age of Hollywood. Found it today while browsing that neighborhood café bookstore, Bibelot Books, and thought of you."

"Ah-hh-h..." she says, both intrigued and delighted that Keegan had thoughts of her today. She feels her body flush with happiness, then rests one hand lovingly across his chest, feeling the warmth of his body rise into the palm of her hand.

He continues, "Interesting reference to what the stars of Golden Age Hollywood had to endure. They often sacrificed their happiness for fame." He opens the book, "Says here, *they were easy fodder for the tabloids and a so-called scandal could ruin a star. So, their lives, manufactured by the studios, were largely fiction.*"

Keegan hands the book to Janet, then slowly stands to stretch. He holds his hand out to her as she jumps to her feet.

"You know," Janet says, still holding the book, "Elaine said the same thing to me a few days ago, how the studios used movie stars and how Hollywood fabricated their life stories. Do you think that's why the grandmother's identity was hidden from Ava all these years?"

With a resigned sigh, Keegan nods, "There's a picture of Ava's parents in the book as well," he adds. He takes the book from Janet and flips through the pages looking for the photos.

"The grandmother's artwork arrived today at Ava's home. Did I tell you the grandmother was an artist? The collection includes a portrait of the Grand Dame herself."

"Does she look like Ava?" Keegan asks, handing the book back to Janet.

"She absolutely does," Janet responds.

"You hungry?" he asks abruptly.

"Sure," Janet answers with wide eyes, confused by the sudden change of topic. She wonders about Keegan's hesitancy to discuss Ava's royal heritage but decides to bring the matter up later in the evening.

Janet enjoys watching Keegan prepare the meal. He works with confidence and a soulful, sound knowledge of when to stir the rice and the exact moment food should be removed from the burner or oven, wearing his well-worn red oven mitts. She listens to his banter with bits of information such as 'For extra flavor, I add garlic butter' and 'Now we will bake it in the oven until it's golden brown and caramelized.' His natural skill and interest in cooking add yet another layer of admiration she has for him.

As they sit down to a plate of steaming vegetables on a bed of wild rice and juicy baked chicken breast, Janet says, "Let's give thanks." She bows her head. With one eye partially open, she sees Keegan bow his head along with her.

"Thanks," he says.

Janet laughs and adds, "Amen."

"Why are you laughing?" Keegan asks.

"Your simplicity is charming," she answers.

"Cheers," he says, clinking his wine glass to hers. "To charming simplicity and good honest food!"

The meal is perfectly seasoned with fresh thyme and tarragon and cooked to mouthwatering perfection. She enjoys a few bites before presenting the question weighing on her earlier in the evening, "May I ask why you seem less than interested in Ava's royal ancestry?"

Keegan finishes another bite of food before answering. "People are people," he sighs. "Even movie stars and people with royal titles. It's who we are on the inside that matters, not our titles, position, fame, or wealth."

"I agree with that," Janet responds. "But don't you find it fascinating and strange that Ava's heritage is a well-kept family secret?"

Keegan looks away, then back at Janet. "Remember when I told you of my wife?"

Janet nods.

"...and how she was impressed with appearances and titles? When we first married, she was pursuing a career as an actress, doing a few local commercials and some modeling jobs. She seemed stable and ambitious. But there came a time when the lines blurred between the real world and an imaginary, superficial one."

Janet picks up her wine glass, taking a sip to relieve some of the tension she is beginning to feel.

"I first noticed her break from reality after mistakenly calling her my 'Meryl Streep.' From then on, she insisted I call her Meryl Streep. She signed letters and notes with *Love, Meryl Streep.*"

"Seems harmless enough. A joke between the two of you? Or, a pet name, perhaps?"

"No. It was more than that. It became her identity. She studied and copied the actress's mannerisms and hairstyles. She always seemed to be acting and looking for a camera, an angle, and posing. She would wave to people as if they were her fans. It was unnerving."

Keegan sighs, picking up his glass and swirling the wine before sipping.

"Later, impulsive spending became an issue. Then there were the frequent mood swings from anger to anxiety. Her behavior seemed erratic. She also began drinking more frequently."

He sets down his wine glass and looks away.

"Once, she was a sophisticated, moderate wine drinker. Later, our refrigerator and cupboards had more wine and liqueurs stored in them than food. She didn't eat much anyway. She had to keep her 'model' figure. Our marriage no longer satisfied her. Eventually, she found someone else."

Janet realizes she is staring at Keegan. She looks down at her plate of half-eaten food, "But you told me on our first date that she married a money manager—nothing about a personality disorder. Sorry to say, but it sounds like she needed help. Counseling, maybe?"

"I was sparing you the depressing details," Keegan says. "She did go for counseling, and we went as a couple for counseling, but she had no interest in saving our marriage. It's hard to relate to someone with extreme mood swings and delusions of grandeur."

Janet remains silent, not wanting to interrupt Keegan's contemplation and painful recollections.

Keegan shifts uneasily in his chair, "Looking back; I'm sure I could have handled the situation better. Soon after our divorce, she married the money manager. I was honestly surprised she found another husband so quickly. However, I did hear through friends that the marriage didn't last."

"What was her real name, if you don't mind me asking?"

Keegan's eyebrows go up as a faint smirk plays around his lips, "Marigold," he answers.

"*Marigold*? Old-fashioned but very sweet," Janet replies with warm sincerity. "Sounds like a character from a Jane Austen novel. Did your wife ever go by a nickname? Goldie, perhaps? There's always Goldie Hawn..."

Keegan shakes his head a resolute 'no.' "It was Meryl Streep she identified with and chose to become. I read somewhere that human character will always fascinate us the most. She certainly was an enigma," he adds quietly.

Janet reaches across the table to cover his hand with hers. "You okay?" she asks. He nods.

"So, please forgive me for showing a bit of restraint regarding Ava's story of royal ancestry. I've experienced enough displays of grandeur and high drama with my ex and a few acquaintances to last a lifetime."

After a moment, Janet stands to help with the dishes.

"No, no... It's fine," he says, slowly rising from his chair to stand beside her.

"Thank you again for the lovely dinner and conversation," she says, gently touching his arm. Then adds, "Mind if I take your book with me? Thinking I might show a few chapters to Ava."

"Yes, yes, I bought it for you," Keegan insists, pressing the book into Janet's hands. "And next time...bring a change of clothes so you can spend the night."

As they embrace and kiss goodnight, a sense of longing and wonder stirs within her. She breathes in the fragrant mixture of woods and robust herbs snipped from his garden earlier this day, scenting his faded blue denim shirt. Janet wants nothing more than to spend this night with Keegan and the night after that as well. To stay with him indefinitely, writing him into the future chapters of her life.

She envisions the two of them living idyllic lives in Keegan's lakeside cottage. A vast profusion of wild roses, pink to deep rose-colored, would grow upon their property, and they would have an herb garden for Keegan's culinary creations as well.

He possessed all the qualities of a romantic leading man: passionate, compassionate, intelligent, and rakishly handsome. *What more could a forty-something-year-old, hopeless romantic ask for?*

Also, Janet considers with a light-hearted smile that *it would be a better commute each day to Ava's mansion.*

CHAPTER THIRTEEN

BAD CHOICES
GOOD INTENTIONS

The weatherman had warned of possible cloud bursts, and now, sure enough, a steady rain beats rhythmically upon the roof of her car as she steers into an open parking space beneath the drooping branches and rain-soaked leaves of an age-old cottonwood.

But not even the rain could dampen her optimistic outlook this morning. Her life was beginning to feel more like a story with an upbeat ending rather than a random series of unfortunate events. A promising long-term relationship with Keegan held a place in her heart as mysteries unraveled with the dawning awareness of her employer's esoteric family heritage. Even Ava, in her own peculiar fashion, was becoming a believer in something greater than herself.

Janet peeks inside her purse to be sure the *Hollywood Legends* book Keegan gave her last night is still there. *Yes, indeed, it is.* Now she will wait for the appropriate time to share it with Ava.

She makes a mad dash toward Ava's house, carrying her to-go coffee cup in one hand while holding her purse protectively overhead with the other, as plans for this new day blossom in her imagination. She glances up. There, standing authoritatively, casting a heavy shadow across the kitchen doorway, is sourpuss Sarah blocking her entrance.

"Ava's waiting for you in the library," the housekeeper says with a huff of impatience, then turns abruptly and walks away.

Janet frowns. With coffee and dripping wet purse still in hand, she heads self-consciously downstairs to the lower level of the home, then follows the windowless hallway back to Ava's library.

Janet spies Ava in a far corner of the room with her knees slightly bent, engaged in some type of activity near a lower-level bookshelf. Curious, Janet pauses to observe Ava removing books from the shelf, one formidable tome at a time, then adding each book to a stack piled knee-deep beside her.

"Good morning," Janet says, just loud enough for Ava to hear as she sets her damp belongings on the nearest glass-top end table. "Are we working in the library this morning?"

Ava straightens her posture, turning in Janet's direction with a look of annoyance. "I want all of these books alphabetized! Can you sort them out? Or maybe I should hire someone *professional* to organize them? Say, someone from that bookstore in town...."

"You mean *Bibelot Books*?" Janet asks.

"Yes. Yes..." Ava answers with an undercurrent of irritation, "World Travels, Religion, Psychology, Scientific studies, and so on...."

"So, you would like them arranged by *category*?" Janet pauses. "Like a bookstore?"

Janet suspects Ava has taken medication to enhance her concentration, for clarity, perhaps? Regardless, she appears uncharacteristically focused and energized in a manic sort of way. Also, she is a bit shaky, as though she has consumed too much caffeine.

Had Ava's doctor prescribed medication based on an emotional reaction Ava had to the shocking discovery of her long-lost grandmother, or is it simply a display of anxiety?

Ava continues removing books from the shelf without reading the spine or cover for title information, then adds them one by one to the stack of books piling higher and now ready to topple. A dozen other books are teetering in a lopsided fashion on an end table, and a half-dozen more books are randomly scattered in disarray across the thick beige carpet. Ava's activity seems wrought with tension, apparently, over nothing more than book categories.

Janet distracts herself from Ava's deterministic chaos by gathering books from the floor, and then finding space for them on a crowded end table as she visually surveys the room.

The windowless library has a subterranean vibe. The glare of glass and metal end tables and four, square leather armchairs have been sparingly added to a far corner of the room. It is a vast space with neutral colors and the lingering scent of stodgy old books, using up a thin amount of oxygen while withstanding the test of time. A distinctly different ambiance from the rest of the modernistic rooms in Ava's home and virtually soundproof, with towering dark mahogany bookcases spanning the room's circumference.

The majestic oil portraits of Ava's celebrity parents prominently displayed between bookcases are incongruous with the room's staid formality. The Hollywood actors' portraits, rich with color and flesh tones, glow with the warmth of human energy. The artist has imbued the paintings with life, capturing the vibrancy of both legend and beauty. Janet's eyes are drawn respectively to each portrait.

Are the spirits of Ava's parents watching her at this very moment? Are thoughts for their only daughter to purposefully move her in the direction of some discovery? Janet wonders.

"I've decided where I will store my grandmother's artwork," Ava says, still focused on the un-shelving of books and avoiding eye contact with Janet.

"That's great," Janet says, trying her best to sound encouraging.

"You can tell Raul we will need his help to move the artwork into the room behind my mother's portrait."

Janet raises her eyebrows in surprise. "But your mother's portrait is between bookcases. I don't see a room."

"You have to lean on the bookcase to open the door, of course," Ava adds impatiently, turning toward Janet to address her directly.

"You want me to move a bookcase?" Janet asks in

confusion and disbelief.

"No, I want you to lean on the bookcase as you move this book forward. That's how you enter the secret room behind it."

Now thoroughly intrigued, Janet glances from Ava to the bookcase, then crosses the room, pointing, "This bookcase?" she asks.

"No, the one beside it, beside my mother's portrait," Ava answers with increasing frustration.

"Well, your mother's portrait is *between* bookcases...oh, never mind...." Janet says as she sidesteps to the neighboring bookcase and leans against it to test it out. The solidly anchored bookcase doesn't budge.

"You have to pull one of the books forward," Ava orders. "The red book, maybe."

Janet leans against the bookcase while pulling the red book forward and simply removes the book from the shelf.

Is this Ava's medication talking?

Janet wonders if she should continue playing along with her employer's illusions.

"No, it's the *other* book. The volume of Shakespeare's plays," Ava insists, now flustered, and obviously confused.

Janet pulls several books forward, each sliding easily off the shelf and into her hands. Finally, she tugs on a classic black and gold-embossed book that resists her pull. She tilts the book toward her in a downward fashion as the bottom corner of the book remains securely fastened to the shelf, then leans into the bookcase.

The bookcase wall swings inward to a dank-smelling room approximately the same dimensions as her downtown studio apartment. She guesses 600 or 700 square feet, but with a fourteen-foot-high (at least) ceiling, housing industrial-sized metal shelving and rolling racks with see-through zippered garment bags holding swirls of fabric pressed inside as if from a secret life. Evening dresses and gowns in a pouf and sweep of silvery black. Some are accented with black tulle and sequined mesh fabric embellished with rhinestones at the neckline, creating a 1930s vintage feel. Fancy, costume-like attire that one might wear to a cocktail party in the Golden Age of Old Hollywood.

The steel shelving is stacked with items in an orderly fashion: a silver candelabra taking up ample space in one corner on a lower shelf and rounded light grayish-brown colored vases with women's and men's faces lightly hand-painted on them with a hauntingly timeworn look. And there are mannequin heads with blonde and red-haired wigs adorned with decorative art deco hair ornaments in bold geometric and zigzag designs. The room could be mistaken for a prop room in the eerie underbelly of a theater. Well...Janet reasons, Ava's parents were actors, after all.

Turning slowly to the middle of the room, Janet takes in the extraordinary collection with breathless fascination. Ava steps unsteadily into the room behind Janet with a book still in hand. Janet follows her employer's gaze to a heightened corner of shelving where the brilliant dazzle of a tiara catches her eye like the flash of a camera.

Janet covers her mouth, trying to maintain her composure as she gasps in surprise. *Is this the same royal headdress featured in the grandmother's portrait?* "It's gorgeous!" she exclaims, unable to contain her amazement. "Is that a stage prop tiara?"

Ava says nothing for a moment. Then looks away. "Ask Raul to bring the artwork downstairs to the library. Have him set it in this storage area, on the floor, and lean it against the shelving", she says, standing directly below the tiara. "See if Elaine is available to help as well. And...oh...find a nice box for the tiara."

Janet feels an eerie sensation breeze through the storage room, sending goosebumps up and down her arms.

The grandmother's portrait is the first piece of artwork Raul carries into the library. He carefully sets it on the floor beside Janet, leaning the portrait against an emptied bookcase. Janet picks up the portrait with the intent of placing it inside the storage room where Ava had indicated but is surprised by its immense weight. Instead, she sets the picture back down with a deep exhale, noticing the unusually thick brown paper backing, and attached legal-sized envelope taped securely to the back of the portrait.

'Oh, dear. Another letter,' Janet sighs in an audible voice without sensing her employer's presence directly behind her.

"What did you find?" Ava demands.

"A brownish legal-sized envelope is attached to the back of your grandmother's portrait. Would you like me to remove it so you can see what's inside the envelope?" Janet asks with a smile that wavers.

Ava lifts her head, uncertain. Her eyes dart around the room, then back to the portrait, "Yes," she says finally, "open the envelope."

Janet carefully peels away the envelope from the brown paper backing and peeks inside. This time to her surprise, it is not a letter, but a photo. She removes the picture holding it low for Ava's viewing.

It is Ava's grandmother in an ivory-colored puffy-sleeved lace dress. Her hair is an upswept pouf of brown with wisps of baby's breath tucked in. She is regally seated in a wing chair as a tuxedoed gentleman wearing a white carnation in his lapel stands glumly beside her. Neither the gentleman nor Ava's grandmother are smiling. Instead, both have a rather cheerless countenance in what appears to be a solemn ceremonial-type setting.

"They all posed like that in those days," Janet says over Ava's shoulder.

"What are you saying?" Ava asks.

"Oh, you know, it appears that they are unhappy, and I was commenting on the style of the day. They all looked miserable in photographs of that era; no one smiled because they had to hold their poses for so long, and it was tiring."

"Hmmm...maybe so," Ava adds, taking the photo from Janet's grasp to examine it more closely.

"See if there's anything written on the back of the photograph," Janet suggests.

Ava reluctantly turns the photo over. "I can't read this scrawl," she says to Janet. "What does it say?"

"Mishka Vasiliev Duchess Zara Romanov Engagement, Finland, 1920," Janet replies.

Ava takes the photograph from Janet, staring hard at the image of her grandmother, then at the image of the gentleman standing beside her grandmother, searching for some physical similarities.

"Who is Mishka Vasiliev?" Ava asks.

"We could do some research and see where it leads," Janet responds. "At least we have their full names and a date to research. We could start from there."

"How would you search for these two people?"

"Oh, I would just type their names and approximate year of birth into that internet search engine, QUERRY. Then, some bit of history might pop up."

"What are you waiting for?" Ava asks.

Janet leaves the library with photo in hand, passing Elaine in the hallway, who looks curiously after her. Janet responds with a hurried sidelong glance waving the photo ever-so-slightly and a shrug, indicating her uncertainty as to the outcome of this new assignment.

Janet has already gathered a bit of history on Ava's grandmother, Duchess Zara, which she skims through on the website. Yes, here are the highlights on QUERRY,

'Duchess Zara Romanov, Russia'

'Born at the turn of the century, Duchess Zara Romanov left Russia with her family in 1916. Duchess Zara was one of about a dozen Russian Romanov relatives who escaped the Bolsheviks and the Russian Revolution of 1917.'

Duchess Zara Romanov, it was noted, 'never married'. She lived out her later years in California working as a landscape artist, deliberately avoiding media attention.

Janet decides to call on Keegan. He's an avid reader, and this is clearly a 'historical' question. Nothing about celebrities or paparazzi in this scenario. He may be of some help...

"Pretty sure he's not famous or wealthy, so this would be a challenge...," Janet begins. "Interested in helping me research a Russian fellow named Mishka Vasiliev, born at the turn of the century? There's a good chance he may be Beverly Rose's father and Ava's grandfather. We found a photo of him with Ava's grandmother, which reads, *Engagement, Finland, 1920.*"

"I'll do it for *you*," Keegan says sweetly. "Also, I find Russian history rather fascinating."

Keegan calls Janet back a half-hour later.

"Not a trace of him, unfortunately," he reports. "I jotted this down, however," he continues. "It's estimated that between 900,000 to two million Russians were able to escape or were expelled by the Soviet government during the 1920s and 1930s."

"So," Janet says, "really no record of him, just a general guess of what might have happened given the historical facts."

"I can keep looking," Keegan offers.

"I'm wondering who contacted Ava to notify her of her grandmother's artwork. Who were they, and what were they to Zara, Beverly Rose, and Ava? And, what happened to all the other belongings her grandmother Zara may have left?"

"Good questions,' Keegan says. "The internet isn't spilling any secrets. That's for sure."

Janet glances up to see Ava lingering in the office doorway with an expression of concern. "What did you find?" Ava asks.

"Gotta go," she says quickly to Keegan, hanging up the phone.

Janet offers Ava the plausible explanation that Mishka Vasiliev and Duchess Zara managed to leave or were expelled by the Soviet government. How they got to Finland is still a mystery, she explains.

"Who were you talking to?" she asks her assistant.

"Keegan!" Janet says with a genuine smile. "We met the night of his uncle's party, um...Gerald Scott. Remember the party I attended with your friend Maxwell Hemingway?"

"You two are dating?" Ava asks with wide eyes.

"Yes, we are," Janet answers. "Bonus, he's a great reader and found an interesting book for us to peruse."

Ava crosses the room to Janet's desk. Janet pulls the book Keegan gave her from her purse and flips to the pages with pictures of Ava's mother and father starring as the glamourous Golden Age of Hollywood 'it' couple.

Janet gently reads a few blurbs about the secretive nature of Hollywood legends. Amazingly, Ava is quiet. She leans in for a closer look as Janet slowly turns the pages.

"Why are you showing me this publicity? I'm well aware of it!" Ava says suddenly, drawing back and waving away the book with a frown.

"The book explains how the big five Hollywood studios insisted on all-American images for their stars. As a result, false backgrounds were created by the studios to create larger-than-life, more glamourous movie stars."

"Still doesn't explain all the secrecy," Ava adds defiantly.

Janet again emphasizes how Hollywood sensationalized their stars to make them appear iconic and excitingly attractive. "A 'no nonsense' background was required. It was all fake, including the staged photo ops. Just more publicity for the next movie. A star became whatever image the studio wanted them to have."

Slowly, Ava begins to understand. "You mean to tell me my mother was forced to hide her family legacy, her mother Zara's true identity?"

Janet nods slowly. "Sadly, yes, I think so. And this may be why your mother valued her friend, Phyllis Hemingway. Phyllis was a reasonable, non-Hollywood person. Honest. Phyllis Hemingway could be trusted."

"But why hide my grandmother's identity from me? I did meet her, of course, but she was introduced to me as a 'family friend'."

"Your mother and father couldn't risk a scandal that might ruin their careers, not to mention your grandmother's and mother's physical safety. The dispiriting truth is that your Russian grandmother was most likely related to the fallen Tzar of Russia. She fled her country – perhaps running for her life - and was living in exile in America."

"I did hear my mother and father speak of the fake, backstabbing Hollywood people, the ones they could not trust."

Janet nods. "They were most likely protecting their careers while at the same time sheltering you from the 'artificial Hollywood' as it was in those days. A scandal could ruin a star's career. So, by hiding your family's identity from you, and the public, they may have been protecting you. Making bad choices with good intentions," Janet says more softly.

"The *Hollywood piranhas,* my parents used to call them."

Ava straightens her posture with a sudden inhale of breath. "Tell Fiona I would like to have my lunch now," she says to Janet lifting her chin in an imperial fashion, before leaving the room.

♦ ♦ ♦

Janet phones Keegan from her desk and tells him with a note of humor in her voice that Ava took the news "with an air of dignity". He suggests she stop by for a happy hour and appetizers at his home. Janet agrees this would be a perfect ending to this most complicated day.

♦　♦　♦

"With heaven looking on, I would like to ask Ava's parents, *what do you want to say to your daughter? Why are you still around?*" Janet says over a glass of wine at Keegan's home later that evening.

"Maybe you should ask..., "Keegan suggests with a wink.

"Contact a medium, you mean?" Janet smiles slowly, uncertain if this is Keegan's wry sense of humor or a serious suggestion.

"I was thinking of a more worldly approach from one of Ava's friends," Keegan says. "What about Phyllis Hemingway? Maybe she knows something?"

"Hmmm...good idea. Think I will suggest to Ava that we connect with Phyllis. I mean, why not?" Janet adds.

Keegan takes Janet by the hand and leads her to the couch, where they cozy up together to watch late-night TV. It had become their comfortable routine.

She ends up staying the night without an extra set of clothes for the next day's work. Just one more routine, she realizes the next morning, that now feels perfectly natural, and, yes, even quite comfortable.

♦　♦　♦

"I would like to reacquaint myself with your guy, Keegan. I remember young Keegan from my earlier days," Ava says to Janet the next morning as she settles into her rolling leather desk chair in their shared lower-level office. Then adds, "Weren't you wearing that same outfit yesterday?"

"Oh, yes. Need to do my laundry," Janet answers, blushing from ear to ear. "And, sure. Keegan would enjoy seeing you again as well. He's a wonderful cook. Maybe he could whip up a delicious dinner for you and Richard to enjoy one of these evenings. Many of his cooking ingredients come straight from his garden!"

Ava tilts her head slightly while considering the offer with a smile that glows from within, then busies herself, shuffling through the mail Elaine has meticulously opened and arranged for her.

Sitting at her desk, Janet stares for an overlong moment before asking, "I've been thinking how we might find out more about your grandmother and wondering if your mother's friend, Phyllis Hemingway, has any information regarding the gentleman in the photo?"

"I told you an art gallery contacted me. And why would I ask Phyllis Hemingway anything?" Ava answers with a retort.

"Your mother thought very highly of Phyllis Hemingway as a genuine friend. Maybe your mother disclosed some of her personal story to Phyllis. That is, of course, if you are still interested in learning more about your mother and grandmother and the gentleman in the photo?"

"Well of course I am," Ava answers with a darting glance.

"Shall I arrange for us to visit Phyllis Hemingway then?" Janet asks.

"She lives in a senior community," Ava says in a more pleasant tone, with a haughty lift of her chin. "Spring Haven retirement community. You will find her by calling the Spring Haven management office. They will connect you to her suite." And suddenly, Ava is smiling. "I like Spring Haven," she says. "I think one day, I will move there."

♦ ♦ ♦

Ava and Janet find Phyllis waiting outside her senior living suite, seated on an upholstered dining room chair beside a burgundy-colored steel rolling walker.

Phyllis' shoulders are rounded, and her head droops a bit, but she has a beautiful well-coifed head of white hair. She lifts her head slightly as they approach, and Janet sees the spark of alertness and intelligence in her aged gray-blue eyes.

"Ava, Ava Fleming! How are you, my dear?" Phyllis asks in a shaky voice.

Ava bends to kiss Phyllis on the cheek. "Lovely to see you again, Phyllis. Is there a place we can talk?"

"I thought we would head to the dining room for a cup of tea," Phyllis answers while reaching for her walker with an unsteady hand. Janet introduces herself then assists by moving the walker within Phyllis' reach.

The three women proceed slowly down a wide hallway passing an in-house beauty salon with a green and white striped decorative awning. Several ladies are having their hair styled, all in a similar fashion. Next, they pass a small grocery store with a red and white striped awning. The senior residence resembles a quaint indoor neighborhood with old-fashioned charm. Finally, the women reach the resident dining hall and sit at a round table with four cushioned dining chairs. Janet spies a tabletop water dispenser dripping with droplets of frosty condensation and a floating medley of lemons, sliced fruit, and ice.

"Please excuse me," she says to her table guests. When Janet returns, balancing three water goblets by their stems, she finds Ava smiling and nodding as Phyllis recounts a story from many years past while resting one feeble hand on Ava's arm.

There is a pause in the conversation as both women turn to watch Janet set the water goblets on the table.

Janet takes the opportunity to ask, "Ava is wondering if you know anything about her grandmother Zara. She's received a shipment of her grandmother's paintings but is not quite sure how the art dealer was able to locate her. Would you possibly have any information to enlighten her?"

"Oh, dear," Phyllis responds, lifting her head with obvious surprise, then squinting slightly to look directly at Ava. "I thought Richard would have told you."

"Told me?" Ava asks, drawing back and straightening in her chair. "Told me what?"

"That your grandmother's estate was left in your name. That's how your mother arranged it with her lawyer. You were to inherit all that your grandmother owned. This much I know."

Ava looks confused. Phyllis continues, "Your mother was trying to protect you all these years from a scandal. Perhaps it backfired."

Phyllis lays a hand again on Ava's arm. "Fame, your mother told me, came at a price. The nature of the business, especially where Hollywood was concerned, drove ambitious, self-centered movie stars to sabotage other actors. Jealousy was a huge factor."

Phyllis takes a slow sip from her water glass, then continues with a weak smile. "Your mother had Cassandra Crawford's husband-that attorney Blackstone-handle the transfer of your grandmother's belongings, which she didn't believe to have much value. Except for your grandmother's paintings, of course."

♦ ♦ ♦

"Why was I not notified of my grandmother's estate, Richard?" Ava asks from the garage/kitchen entrance, her face reddening with anger. "You can imagine my embarrassment when I had to learn of my grandmother's inheritance from Phyllis Hemingway!"

Janet stands awkwardly beside Ava as Richard stands motionless before them. It was unusual for Richard to be home midday and more uncommon for him to be greeting his wife at the kitchen entrance. This fact doesn't seem to faze Ava.

"You were at Canyon Ranch when the documents arrived," Richard replies. He stands quietly, closing his eyes and taking a calm breath before continuing. "I know how much you dislike legal paperwork, Ava. I also thought the shock of discovering your grandmother's history might be a bit much, so I returned the documents to Nigel Blackstone. He's agreed to review the documents with you privately."

It is then that Janet notices Richard's facial tic. He blinks hard.

"The contract is in that specialized language of the legal profession," Richard explains, "and Nigel is simplifying the language for you. Crossing out the 'therefores' and 'theretos'."

Ava isn't listening. Instead, she glances about the room looking for someone or something to vent her anger on.

"We are not talking a huge fortune here, Ava. Just some odds and ends and a contract for those paintings," Richard adds with a small open-palmed gesture.

Ava looks directly at Richard, her voice rising with a bitter edge. "You didn't think I'd want to know this information immediately, if not sooner, *Richard*? Why does everyone assume I am incapable of handling these types of matters? I've made it this far, haven't I?" Ava says, shaking her head in disapproval. "My grandmother's identity hidden from me all these years, and now *this*? It's almost too much to bear. Who can I trust? Anyone? Hollywood was fake—but what about the rest of you? Are you all *fake people*, too?"

Richard looks down at the floor without answering his wife. Janet surmised during her brief time working for Ava that her employer's life had not been a 'normal' one by any stretch of the imagination. After their daughter's brain injury, Ava's parents made sure she was well cared for. Her life had been a series of pampered indulgences. Would she even understand a legal document? The legalese alone would baffle her.

"And now, I must excuse myself before I say or do something I will most certainly regret," Ava says in a tone of high moral indignation as she leaves the room.

Ava's dramatic exit, while completely serious, seems a bit overdone, and Janet wonders if there isn't a latent talent for acting that Ava hasn't fully explored.

Richard and Janet are left alone in the kitchen, looking uncomfortably at each other. Finally, Richard hangs his head, shaking it hopelessly. Janet watches Richard's reaction sympathetically for a moment before excusing herself.

◆　◆　◆

"Well, looks like it's up to the attorney to explain things to Ava," Janet says to Keegan later that evening.

Janet and Keegan are seated on the couch, enjoying their usual glass of wine. Keegan has also prepared a platter of cheeses, fruits, and crackers. The local news is on.

Keegan picks up the remote control and lowers the volume. "What's that you say now?" he asks.

"Nigel Blackstone, Cassandra Crawford's husband, is holding Ava's documents for her. He will explain the inheritance to her in simpler terms."

"What's so complicated about a signature?" Keegan asks. "She signs on the dotted line and gets to keep the paintings, right?"

Janet nods.

"You mentioned earlier that Richard told Ava there wasn't anything of value left in Zara's estate? Right? So, why the fuss?"

Janet taps lightly on her wine glass. "Seems suspicious, doesn't it?" She sips her wine before continuing. "Do you think there is reason to believe that Zara's estate has more value? Why is everyone tiptoeing around these documents?"

Keegan leans back into the comfort of his leather sofa with a swooshing sound, "Maybe this has more to do with the treasure hidden within Ava's Rococo nightstand? Who gets to keep the heirloom necklace, for instance?"

"Well, Ava gets to keep the necklace, of course. It's been passed down from Grandmother to mother to daughter. It's part of her royal legacy. Whatever its history, it belongs to Ava."

"Like you belong to me?" Keegan asks, reaching for Janet and pulling her close. "Maybe the necklace has some kind of magical power," he says playfully, "like you have over me."

Suddenly, they are both laughing at the happiness of this moment and the thought of an old-fashioned fairy tale ending, not only for Ava but for each other as well.

CHAPTER FOURTEEN
LADY MACBETH

When Janet arrives for work the next morning, she finds the Fleming family attorney, Nigel Blackstone, seated on the orange corduroy couch and Ava, adjacent to him, in the orange corduroy swivel chair. Ava is energized. Her eyes are glowing. She enjoys hobnobbing with Diamond Lake's upper crust, even if it is a 'business meeting' with her attorney.

Nigel clears his throat, straightening a few loose papers on the coffee table. "Cassandra has a new piece of jewelry for you to view," he tells Ava, then reaches into his briefcase for a file folder of paperwork.

Ava straightens her shoulders and back. "Tell her to call me," she says with a fresh look of excitement.

Odd place to conduct an attorney-client session, Janet thinks to herself. But Janet knows Ava is most comfortable in her own home, on this corduroy furniture with a full-on view of both the kitchen and Diamond Lake, and of course, with staff around to cater to her particular needs.

Ava calls to her assistant when she sees her standing in the entryway. "Janet, Nigel is asking how many paintings arrived the other day?"

Fiona appears from the kitchen with a tray of steaming coffee cups, sugar, and cream. She removes items from the tray with great care setting them before Ava and Nigel on the coffee table before exiting the room.

"Eighteen paintings and the oil portrait. So, a total of nineteen," Janet replies.

"Your mother had a contract with the California art gallery, *ENVISION*," Nigel says. "You just need to sign the last page of each section to acknowledge receipt of your grandmother's paintings."

"We obviously received them," Ava responds with mild annoyance, shaking her head. "I arranged this with the gallery owner before they were shipped to my home."

"It's just a bit of paperwork that needs to be processed. Your mother had an arrangement with the California art gallery to display some of your grandmother's paintings and hold the others in storage," Nigel continues. "I understand the art dealer charged you a fee for storing, displaying, and shipping your grandmother's paintings to you."

"That's correct, but the paintings do not flow well with the style of my home," Ava explains with a dismissive wave. "I'm more a fan of modern abstract art. My grandmother's artwork is contemporary but of landscapes and such," she glances at Janet with a look of smug superiority. "So, I'm just keeping them in storage for now," Ava adds. "Not sure what will become of those paintings."

"I'm guessing the paintings were mostly of sentimental value to your mother," Nigel suggests.

"Perhaps," Ava says, leaning forward unceremoniously to sign the documents.

"This contract is for you to file and keep," Nigel explains. "The other contract is for me to hold onto."

"Janet, please place this contract on my desk," Ava says, holding the file folder out to Janet.

As Janet heads downstairs, file folder in hand, she overhears Ava ask Nigel, "What is Cassandra doing today? Can I meet with her?"

To be safe, Janet sneaks a peek at the contents of the folder before setting it on Ava's desk. There is a good chance Ava will misplace the folder and ask about it at some point. The top paper reads CONTRACT and names the California art gallery, *ENVISION, Palm Springs, CA*, and Beverly Rose Fleming as holder and executor of Zara Romanoff's artwork.

Later that afternoon...

"You're going to drive me to a meeting in downtown Minneapolis. We'll be leaving soon. Have Elaine open my jewelry vault," she tells Janet through the office intercom.

♦ ♦ ♦

Ava stares straight ahead, holding her purse on her lap as Janet drives them to the downtown meeting. She drives Ava's silver Mercedes into an underground parking ramp as Ava directs, then hands the keys over to the parking garage valet. They take the elevator to the street-level lobby. When they disembark from the elevator, they are standing before a swanky downtown jewelry store with circular columns reaching a twenty-foot-high ceiling with crystal chandeliers and a series of scrolled open brass ironwork gates that Janet assumes double as gated security when the store is closed.

A saleswoman quickly approaches. "Wonderful to see you again, Ava," she says with raised eyebrows and a lingering touch on Ava's arm.

The saleswoman coaxes her client to the jewelry counter. Ava steps lightly when the saleswoman offers to clean her wedding rings. She slides her massive 4-carat diamond ring and wedding band off, handing them over, then pulls a rectangular brown box from her purse as the saleswoman turns her back. Janet recognizes the box as the one recently acquired on the day of her appointment with Cassandra Crawford.

The saleswoman returns with Ava's rings which now sparkle with renewed brilliance.

"I would like earrings to compliment this exquisite necklace," she tells the sales clerk while lifting the jewelry box lid.

"Oh, that's quite lovely, my dear," the sales clerk says with exaggerated interest.

"Yes, it's a customized piece. Made just for me," Ava adds, her eyes fixated on the amethyst pendant.

"May I suggest showy drop dangle amethyst earrings in a gold setting," the clerk advises. "Amethyst has a beauty all its own, and the gold setting would have the vintage look and feel of jewelry from the 1920s."

Ava's eyes brighten as she leans in over the jewelry counter. The saleswoman continues with her sales pitch.

"Amethyst is a power stone, and it's quite affordable."

Ava jerks her head back suddenly. "What do you mean

by 'quite affordable'?"

"It's a semi-precious stone with a hardness score of 7, which makes amethyst an excellent choice for vintage jewelry. You'll have it for a lifetime."

Ava turns her head away as if in thought. "What would you value this necklace at?" she finally asks.

"Well, if you like, we can have a jeweler appraise the necklace for you," the sales clerk replies with a satisfied smile.

"Yes. That is what I will do then," Ava answers.

The clerk takes the box from Ava and writes up an order, finally handing over a receipt. "We should have an estimate ready for you this week sometime, along with a proposed design for your new earrings. I'll give you a call when both are ready."

Ava says nothing. She stuffs the receipt in her purse, then wanders across the aisle to another jewelry counter, distracted by all the glittering baubles elegantly displayed under glass.

Janet stands at attention with a watchful eye on her employer, unsure of her next move. *Should she hasten her employer to the door? Should she encourage her to arrive at the previously mentioned meeting? Or was the word 'meeting' used as a clever ruse to announce to staff that she was working when in fact, she wanted Janet to drive her to the flashy downtown jewelry store?*

Janet decides to wait patiently as Ava stands poised above the jewelry case, completely absorbed in the luster of fine jewelry. Janet then drives her employer directly home.

◆　◆　◆

"What a day," she tells Keegan over the phone later that evening. "All that build-up and drama over a contract that required nothing more than a few signatures."

"How's that?" Keegan asks.

"Well, the contract names a California art gallery, *ENVISION,* and Beverly Rose Fleming as holder and executor of Zara Romanoff's artwork. So, Ava just needed to sign and acknowledge receipt of her grandmother's paintings." Janet gives a catlike stretch. "My guess is that Ava's mother would decide what to do with the artwork at some point but felt conflicted, and therefore never got around to sending for her mother Zara's paintings."

"You mean, the paintings sat in the art gallery for several years?"

"Yes. I overheard Nigel tell Ava that some of the paintings were occasionally displayed, but none ever sold," Janet adds. "They're really quite beautiful, and the oil portrait of her grandmother is of museum quality."

"So, I have an idea," Keegan says. "Let's change the subject."

Janet laughs. "Sorry, didn't realize I was rambling on again about Ava."

"I propose you request a few weeks off to visit my Palm Springs condo with me. I need to check on it occasionally, and I was hoping you would make the trip with me."

"What? When? Me?" Janet responds with a sudden burst of delight.

"Sure. Ask Ava. I have a hunch she likes you more than she lets on. I know she trusts you."

"Hmmm... I'm thinking," Janet answers.

Keegan was right in saying that Ava trusted her. In addition, Janet suspected that Ava enjoyed an adventurous love story, possibly from all those years of watching the romance movies her mother and father starred in. *Hadn't Ava asked just the other day to meet the 'new boyfriend'?*

It was worth a shot anyway.

◆　◆　◆

Next morning....

Janet has every intention of speaking with Ava first thing this morning. She's prepared an intro that includes Keegan dropping by with one of his signature dishes around dinnertime. Hopefully, Ava will be able to glean from the meet-up that Janet and Keegan are a mature couple with good intentions. Janet believes this will build a foundation of trust for Janet's future employment with Ava and for Janet and Keegan as a couple within the Diamond Lake community.

Stepping into Ava's home this early morning, she is greeted with the irresistible aroma of freshly brewed coffee and pauses in the kitchen for a quick refill. Just as she is topping off her Caribou coffee, she senses a presence behind her. She turns abruptly to see Ava approaching in a loosely belted flowing white robe with one arm stretched out before her. Ava reaches for Janet with a look of fright.

"Oh, Janet, Janet," Ava calls out. "Last night, my mother appeared to me."

Suddenly speechless, Janet holds her coffee cup motionless in midair.

Ava continues, "Mother, mother, I said reaching out to her... but she backed away. What is it? I asked her. Why are you here? My mother answered in a ghost-whispered voice, '*You know why I am here. Look within your heart*'."

Ava looks at Janet with a skittish, watery gaze. "But I don't know," I say to my mother. I honestly don't know. When I woke up, my heart was racing. What is my mother trying to tell me? Is she angry with me? She seemed angry!"

"Honestly," Janet answers, "Ghost conversations can be so vague." She then feels a twinge of regret for responding too quickly.

"Oh," Ava says with confusion and obvious disappointment, "Is my mother angry or sad?! Is she in pain?"

"Maybe your mother's spirit is upset about something you have no control over," Janet suggests.

"Like, what, for instance?"

"Some secret or feeling she still carries, trapped inside her. What becomes of our memories, secrets, and regrets once we pass? *It's not so much what we leave behind, but who we leave behind that matters*," Janet answers, quoting a line from Beverly Rose's letter.

"Maybe it has something to do with that man in the photo..." Ava offers.

"You mean Mishka Vasiliev?" Janet asks.

"Yes. Maybe Mishka was left behind."

Janet nods slowly, "Left behind as in a lost love? A wandering soul? Is this what you are thinking?"

And then, in this most fortuitous of moments, Janet suggests that her mother's appearance may have something to do with the mysterious Rococo nightstand, situated right beside her bed each night as she sleeps.

"Why that?" Ava asks.

"Well, since your mother appeared to you while you

were sleeping, the answer may be intertwined with your dreams. The cabinet has a family history, and it's been kept close to you all these years."

"So, what secrets would be hidden away from me?"

"Maybe your mother wants to show you the '*real woman*' she was, not the version Hollywood created."

A long moment passes, and despite Ava's anxiety over the frightful dream, she asks Janet to follow her back to the bedroom. Ava tells Janet to open the lower doors of the nightstand, then bends low from the waist to peer inside the cabinet and sees a glint of light, a sparkle of cobalt blue enamel.

"What's that?" she asks her assistant, pointing to the far interior corner of the nightstand.

"Would you like me to investigate?" Janet asks.

"Yes," Ava answers ever so faintly.

Janet tugs the false wall forward and then removes the cobalt blue enamel box. She hands the box to Ava. Ava lifts the lid with a sudden inhaled gasp of air, drops the box, then sinks to her knees upon the plush bedroom carpet, her head cushioned by the side of the bed.

◆ ◆ ◆

"So, did you have a chance to ask Ava for a couple of weeks off to visit my Palm Springs condo?" Keegan asks Janet later that evening.

"I'll answer that in a moment, but first, I must tell you the real drama of this morning," Janet says with a fluttery feeling of excitement in her stomach.

"I'm stopping to top off my coffee with the housekeeper's fresh brew when Ava, starring as Lady

Macbeth, enters the kitchen from stage left. Like the famous sleepwalking scene from Shakespeare's tragedy Macbeth. Ava is floating in a type of trance, convinced that her mother had visited her in a dream - which led us to discover the Duchess Zara's necklace and documents hidden within the Rococo nightstand!"

"Really?!" Keegan asks with a shock of surprise. "So now, what happens to the diamond necklace?"

"Wait, wait...I didn't tell you that Ava almost lost consciousness after opening the Fabergé box. She literally collapsed to the floor! I had to help her to her feet. It was all very dramatic and sensational."

Janet then lowers her voice. "And, oh yes, the necklace... Elaine told me they are arranging to have it appraised and insured."

"And Maxwell's inheritance, how did she take that?"

"She looked bewildered, of course, when she saw the legal documents, then said she would pass them along to her attorney, Nigel Blackstone."

"You had quite a day, my dear!" Keegan says.

"Yes, I did," Janet replies, taking a deep breath, "and since I didn't have the opportunity to discuss our travel plans with her, I thought you might be open to stopping by tomorrow evening with one of your homemade fresh-from-the-garden meals for Richard and Ava. We can tell Ava of our travel plans over dinner."

With eyes closed, Janet envisions the details of her newly imagined plan. "Now, the thing is, the gallery that stored Zara's paintings is also in Palm Springs. So, I plan to copy both sides of the photo, of Duchess Zara and Mishka, to bring with us, then present it to the owner of the *ENVISION* art gallery. See if the owner offers any ancestral or historical information. You know, some detective work. Might be a fun bit of detective work, don't you think?"

"How does Ava feel about this?" Keegan asks warily.

"Not sure I'll tell Ava my plan," Janet hesitates midsentence, "maybe I'll just wait and see how it all shakes out, you know, if any history pops up or whatever. When the facts become evident, then all will be revealed."

♦ ♦ ♦

Ava turns into an almost playful version of herself when she sees Keegan the following evening. She teases him about his casual appearance. "Wonder what your Uncle Gerald would say about your sporty clothes and pickup truck?" she asks.

Keegan laughs it off as he sets the stoneware crock pot on the kitchen counter.

"Oh, my Uncle Gerald is well aware of my Indiana Jones image. He might even be a bit envious. And it's not a pickup truck. It's a recreational vehicle. Perfect for my recreational lifestyle!" he laughs.

Keegan removes the heavy ceramic lid from the pot. The light, smoky woodiness of cedar-plank salmon and vibrant lemon and tarragon for a simple side dish of hot blanched green beans fill the room with delicious aroma. Even Richard seems duly impressed with Keegan's meal presentation and selection of herbs harvested from the garden.

"Won't you be joining us for dinner?" Ava asks, looking up at Keegan and ignoring Janet.

"No, the meal is portioned for you and Richard, but

Janet and I will join you with a glass of wine if that sounds good?"

Keegan and Janet busy themselves setting silverware and serving utensils, wine, and water glasses as Ava and Richard take their seats at the table.

"So, where do you vacation during these dreary Minnesota winter months?" Richard asks Keegan while reaching for his glass of wine.

"I have a condo in Palm Springs," Keegan answers.

"Oh," Ava says with surprise, "I have a condo there as well!"

"It so happens," Keegan adds, "that Janet and I were talking about visiting Palm Springs together. We'd be happy to check on your condo while we are there."

Ava appears to have taken Keegan's suggestion in stride. "Well, no need, really. I have a man who oversees the property. A big Swede named Lars. I am, however, wondering how the weather in Palm Springs is this season...

We haven't been to my Palm Springs home in ages." Ava turns to Richard for confirmation. "We haven't been there in a while, right Richard?"

Richard nods.

"When were you thinking of going to Palm Springs? You could go sooner rather than later," Ava suggests, delighted and surprised by her own sudden burst of generosity and spontaneity.

"That's a great idea!" Keegan quickly adds, brimming with enthusiasm.

Janet and Keegan share a look as if they've just won the lottery jackpot.

CHAPTER FIFTEEN

ENGAGEMENT. FINLAND. 1920

One week later...

"Well, there you have it," Keegan says, turning to Janet. "That highway stretching below us is the road to my condo. Only about a forty-five-minute drive from the airport."

Janet leans across Keegan's lap to look out the airplane window at the barren landscape below. "You mean that one narrow road is the main highway?" She smiles. "These are the kind of driving directions that work for me! Just follow that straight black line to your destination, Ma'am!"

"And now, we're flying over the shopping district along Palm Canyon Drive, where a great Italian restaurant and the *ENVISION* art gallery are located."

Janet grabs Keegan's arm as the plane descends, and he laughs, placing one hand over hers for reassurance.

WELCOME TO PALM SPRINGS, the overhead sign in

the PSP airport reads.

The airport is a postage stamp compared to other airports she's traveled through. Super cute, though, with outdoor hallways and patios all located right within the airport.

As they step outside into the warmth and light of California desert air, she begins to float upon a calming wave of relaxation. On the far horizon looms a big mountain view. The earth-colored mountains look as foreign as moon rocks to her. *Too muddy-pie brown and desolate*, she thinks to herself. *Where's the green stuff? The trees? The grass?*

But then, the tall desert palms and low cactus plants catch her eye. Spiky groundcover cactus showcasing hearty flourishes of flowers in varying shades of pink. *Pink, her favorite color.* She realizes it will take some time to adjust her northern hemisphere sense of beauty to the desert landscape and wildlife. Still, she is impatient to begin her adventure with Keegan in the Sonoran Desert of southern California.

They rent a car, and it's a smooth, effortless drive for twenty-some straight miles along Interstate 10.

"Where is everyone?" she asks as the security gate rises to allow entrance into a sprawling community of single-story ranch-style homes. The homes are long and narrow, white or beige colored with red-tiled roofs and flat green lawns with palm trees.

They pass two large community pools of serene greenish-blue water that glimmer in the sunlight. No swimmers splashing about, and no sunbathers lounging around either of the pools. Not a soul in sight.

"Is this the off-season?" Janet asks.

"You'll find Palm Springs is very laid back," Keegan answers, reaching for his sunglasses.

"When my ex and I decided to buy in Palm Springs, she thought we would enjoy a country club atmosphere. Hollywood stars like Frank Sinatra and Elvis Presley had homes here. Many celebrities still maintain homes in Palm Springs. She didn't consider that their homes were built for privacy, intended as celebrity hideaways. The high white stucco walls you see around some of the homes are intentional."

"What about you? Why did you decide to buy here?"

"I thought it would be a nice winter vacation getaway. Easy to get to. There's the clubhouse," Keegan says with a nod as they drive past an eye-catching one-level structure with a terra cotta tile roof. "Hiking and biking trails. Great for recreational activities, although it can be scorching hot here in the summer."

"I wonder why Ava doesn't use her Palm Springs condo more often?" Janet asks.

"Probably too boring for her," Keegan shrugs. "Same as my ex-wife. Too relaxing for those high energy, social butterfly types."

Keegan's 'condo' is a detached residence—more of a home, really, with a white stucco exterior. The space is light and bright inside the house, with high ceilings, ceiling fans, and a spacious private courtyard patio off the kitchen.

"There's only one bedroom," Keegan says, raising his eyebrows with a questioning gaze. "Would you like to see it?"

Janet knows exactly what Keegan is implying and what *she* wants. She slides her hand into his and gently tugs on his arm with a sparkle of suggestion in her eyes. "I believe you said the bedroom is this way."

Her senses deepen as she inhales the pure desert air whirring under the ceiling fan and Keegan's rousing musky wood signature scent.

Think I'm going to like Palm Springs, she smiles to herself.

♦ ♦ ♦

Keegan's favorite Italian restaurant is just one city block from the *ENVISION* art gallery.

They stroll into the gallery after dinner and find other after-dinner tourists casually browsing a crowded collection of eclectic artworks. A man and woman are speaking quietly to one another over a colorful twist of a four-foot-high metal sculpture. Another couple, two men, are standing across the room for a better perspective of the hanging wall art.

In a far corner of the store, is a middle-aged man in a lilac-colored dress shirt and white linen pants leaning against a glass countertop. Flipping through a large book, he occasionally glances up to survey the store's activities. Janet nudges Keegan as she pulls the photo of Duchess Zara and Mishka from her purse, then nods toward the man at the counter.

Although not a dead ringer for Mishka, it is the same attractive face with full dark eyebrows and look of determination.

"Let's ask him about Zara's paintings for an opener. I'll do the talking," Janet says, approaching the man with amped-up energy.

"Excuse me, are you the owner?"

"Yes," the man says, closing the book, then straightening as he turns to face Janet.

"I'm interested in the landscape pictures you displayed a while back. Painted by a Russian woman."

"Could you be more specific?" he asks.

"Well, I'm Ava Fleming's assistant," Janet pauses, searching the man's face for name recognition. "You shipped paintings to the Minnesota home of Ava Fleming about a month ago?"

The man frowns, "was there a problem with the paintings?" he asks.

"Oh no, no, nothing like that!" Janet adds quickly.

"Ava Fleming is simply interested in any background information you might have on the painter.

Duchess Zara, you see, was her grandmother, and she knew very little about her."

The store owner stands quietly, studying Janet.

"I've seen bios for painters that accompany their artwork," she continues. "Anything like that, say, a sheet of paper that I might show my employer would be most helpful."

The owner gives her a quick smile. "Sorry, no bio for that artist. Her daughter left the artwork with us. So, we never had much background on the artist, although her landscapes were lovely and admired by many of the gallery's visitors."

Janet presents the photo of Zara and Mishka. "Does this photo seem familiar to you?"

He takes the photo with widening eyes and quietly stares momentarily before answering, "My great-uncle,

Mishka. Why... or how did you come by this picture?"

"It was sealed to the back of Duchess Zara's oil portrait."

"My family has photos of my great-uncle Mishka, but none with this woman. Hmmm...how authentic is this photo?" he asks.

"Turn the picture over," Janet says.

The owner turns the copied photo over and reads the longhand inscription, faded with time.

"Mishka Vasiliev
Duchess Zara Romanov
Engagement, Finland, 1920"

Janet waits a few moments, watching the man's face for a reaction before asking, "We are wondering most of all about Mishka V. What happened to Mishka V., the man pictured with Duchess Zara?"

He shifts from foot to foot while holding the photo.

"You mentioned that Mishka Vasiliev was your great-uncle," Janet adds.

"I'm guessing that you are just asking for some family history?"

Janet nods 'yes'. Several minutes pass as he waits for the last two browsers to leave his store.

"Well, the story I've been told is that Mishka was traveling in Europe when the Russian Revolution of 1917 threatened the safety of his family still living in Russia."

With a downcast expression, he looks at the photo in his hands before continuing. "Mishka returned to Russia to take his widowed mother and two sisters to safety. To get them out of the country. This was a dangerous trip for him to make. He traveled by train part of the way, then traveled with them in darkness by sleigh through snow-covered woods crossing into Finland. Eventually, thanks to my great-uncle Mishka, the family of four made it safely to America, and here we are today, in modern times living in Palm Springs, CA. This is where *I was* born."

"So, Mishka V was a hero?"

The owner looks from Keegan to Janet before answering.

"Yes, you could certainly say that. But he died broken-hearted, without ever finding his young fiancée. While in Finland, he met a beautiful woman. Mishka wouldn't say much about her, and he passed away with a sad kind of loneliness and emptiness.

What did you say your connection is to this photo?" he asks with a raised voice and a quick glance at Janet.

"I work for the movie star Beverly Rose Fleming's daughter, Ava Fleming. We believe the man in the photo may have been Beverly Rose Fleming's father."

"Ahhh....how interesting! The beautiful Beverly Rose Fleming! I remember the day she walked into our gallery. I was amazed by her stunning emerald-green eyes. She made a modest request to store and perhaps occasionally display some of her mother's paintings. Later, she added the magnificent oil portrait to the collection, which she had commissioned. We were instructed not to sell any of the paintings. Eventually, she told us she would send for them. But not yet. The time was not quite right."

Janet and Keegan look at each other in disbelief. "Wow, what are the chances?" Janet asks.

"So, are you saying the woman in this photo was my great-uncle Mishka's fiancée?"

"Yes, it appears so," Keegan answers.

"What a strange twist of fate that Beverly Rose would walk into your gallery of all the art galleries she could have chosen," Janet says in amazement.

"Yes, I once asked her about that in a manner of conversation. What made her pick this gallery to store and display her mother's artwork? I'll never forget her answer. She told me she was drawn to the gallery when she saw it from across the street. Our small white building had an aura of mystery that intrigued her, so she crossed the street, entered our gallery, and introduced herself.

Later, she said that perhaps it was on a whim that she chose our gallery, but now, who's to say?" The owner shrugs.

He hands the photo back to Janet. "Any chance I could have a copy of this photo? I know my family would be very interested in seeing it."

"Of course," Janet replies. "I'd be happy to have a copy made for you."

"Now you've brought a bit of magic to my great-uncle Mishka's story. I believe somewhere in the spirit world, he is smiling."

"You have been extremely helpful," Janet says, shaking the man's hand earnestly. "Thank you so very much for your time. What did you say your name was?"

"I didn't," he answers with a smile. "It's Mishka. Mishka Petrov, that is."

Janet lets out a startled laugh. "That's incredible!"

Keegan steps forward, shaking Mishka Petrov's hand affectionately with a light squeeze. "Wonderful to meet you, Mishka Petrov."

As they step back outside onto the sidewalk, Keegan

turns to Janet, "I wonder why Beverly Rose had her mother's artwork displayed if she didn't want to sell it? Seems an odd request."

"Is it possible that Beverly Rose was caught somewhere between living the make-believe life of a Hollywood legend and a runaway Russian royal? Maybe *she* wondered who *she* was?" Janet answers.

"Sure. Makes sense. She was struggling with her identity," Keegan adds.

Janet nods reflectively. "Perhaps the desire to showcase her mother's talent and later commission the oil portrait of Duchess Zara in all its outrageous splendor, royal Fabergé jewels, tiara, diamond necklace and all, was her way of unveiling the truth, the history and beauty of her mother, the artist's soul?"

CHAPTER SIXTEEN

SPIRITUAL CONNECTIONS

Later that week...

Mishka's eyes light up as Janet and Keegan present him with a copy of the photo. "My family was interested to hear your story," he says in a rush of words. "At first, not believing me. Then my aunt Nadia, in a blur of remembrance, checked the family album and found she had the same photo!"

Janet looks to Keegan for his reaction, but he is staring directly at Mishka Petrov in anticipation of hearing more.

"This photo opened the floodgates of my aunt Nadia's memories, of stories passed along by *her* mother."

Mishka glances toward the door, pausing as the letter carrier crosses the room, laying mail on the glass countertop. "Thank you," he says to the mailman, then waits for him to exit the art gallery before continuing with his story.

"Well, as I was saying, she told of my great-uncle Mishka Vasiliev and how '*he learned to suffer,*' which I thought was an interesting turn of phrase. Aunt Nadia told us how Mishka sacrificed for his family when he returned to Russia on a rescue mission, saving his mother and sisters from the Bolshevik revolutionaries. He brought them to safety in Finland; then, they crossed the Atlantic to America. Sailing over the Atlantic Ocean was rough. He was often seasick from the turbulence and salty air. First landing in New York, then later to the sunshine state of California for health reasons."

Mishka Petrov looks at the photo in his hands with a kind of melancholy for the fading memory of his great-uncle. "According to his two sisters, their brother kept this picture bedside in a silver frame as he convalesced. He believed - as did his sisters – that he would soon recover and return to his fiancée. But sadly, that wasn't meant to be."

The store owner pauses to sit on a high wooden stool near the counter before continuing.

"Her real name was not Beverly Rose Fleming, you know," Mishka Petrov adds, "that's all made-up Hollywood stuff. Her real name was Tasha Romanov. Beverly Rose, or should I say Tasha Romanov, shared some information with me after adding the oil portrait to her mother's art collection. She commissioned the oil portrait to reclaim her birthright, and her mother's birthright, which she felt was stolen when Hollywood reinvented her. Funny, I never imagined the connection between us. I mean between our families. I think I was holding back...waiting to discover more."

"She shared this private information with you?" Janet asks with an incredulous stare. "Beverly Rose must have truly had a change of heart. So many secrets. She must have grown tired of pretending to be someone she was not."

Fumbling for words, Janet looks briefly at Keegan for assurance that what she is hearing is true, then adds, "How grateful my employer, Ava Fleming, will be to hear the story of her mother, grandmother, and grandfather and to know this period of her family's history."

Mishka Petrov looks at Janet with a weak smile. "I'm afraid my family isn't interested in meeting with Ava. 'Too many painful memories,' as they say. Just thought I would mention this in case you asked."

"I understand," Janet says, swallowing hard. "I have a friend who was adopted but never had a strong interest in meeting her birth parents. I believe she felt the same way; too many painful memories. Let the past rest in the past."

"Thank you for understanding. I have a business in Palm Springs, and my family is embedded in the community. One can never predict how this information will be misused or misunderstood."

"It will be our secret and Ava's," Janet says with quiet melancholy looking Mishka directly in the eyes and clasping his hand.

"Also, nice meeting you, "Keegan adds, shaking the shop owner's hand.

After walking out of the store and down the block, Janet turns to Keegan, "Why would Beverly Rose Fleming reveal her true identity to the art gallery owner? She barely knew him."

"Her domineering husband, Sebastian, had passed, and she was a widow in her later years. Maybe she believed it was time to be open and truthful," Keegan answers as they continue in a slow, meditative walk. "Or maybe, she felt a kind of spiritual connection to her cousin's family."

"Maybe so, but she could have revealed more to her daughter. And can you believe the Petrov family doesn't even want to correspond with Ava!"

"Janet," Keegan responds, stopping suddenly with a double take of surprise, "you just told us your friend wasn't interested in meeting her birth parents!"

"I know. But that's different. My friend's family heritage isn't based on a fairy tale romance like Ava's grandmother and grandfather. Ava is the offspring of Russian royalty, for crying out loud!"

"Well, I'm just saying that your friend's mother also has a story. Maybe not descended from Russian royalty but some version of it." Keegan reaches for Janet's hand, giving it a playful squeeze. "I bet if we searched back far enough, we would find that we all have a fascinating past."

Janet raises her eyes, looking off at the distant big mountain view, "Beverly Rose did write in her letter '*that it's not so much what we leave behind, but who we leave behind that matters.*' Maybe that prop necklace from the movie *FOREVER* is the most valuable piece of jewelry Ava will ever own. So, my question is do we ever really leave those we love behind, or they with us (forever) in spirit? And what of the wandering spirits, the lost loves of our lives that haunt the rooms of our homes? Do they seek to reunite with us? Are they patiently waiting until we, too, become spirit and join them?"

They turn down a narrow street, and Keegan slows his pace. "Is this about the ghost we saw in Ava's home that night?"

Janet squints into the sunlight. "Well, sure it is. How could it *not* be?" she asks.

"Maybe we are not meant to interfere in the spiritual realm or deliver an inspirational message to Ava. Maybe we are just meant to pass along the stories as we've heard them. Introduce Ava to her grandmother and grandfather and let the family, both past and present, make their telepathic connections. Could this be what you are thinking?" he gently asks.

"What I'm thinking," Janet says with a deep, satisfied breath, "is how grateful I am for you. Thankful that you are here with me now, exploring both past and present. That you believe in myth and magic, and really, what were the chances of me, the lonely New York widow, meeting the sensitive and intelligent man that you are?"

Janet stops and stands beside Keegan with an upturned face. "If I were to die right now," she says with a watery gleam in her eyes, "I'd be by your side as you work in the garden. Lounge on your lakeside deck. Sit across from you at the dinner table each night, and later, when you sleep, I'd stroke your face with a loving whispery touch to let you know I'm with you, watching over you."

With a weightless gaze, Keegan looks into Janet's eyes and smiles *thank you.*

Then, without another word, they kiss a kiss that holds no doubt of their devotion to one another. A statement of love that defies explanation.

CHAPTER SEVENTEEN

YOU'RE MY ANGEL

A va sends Janet out in her silver Mercedes to pick up the amethyst necklace she's had appraised at the swanky downtown Minneapolis jewelry store.

The sales associate politely greets Janet, peering over her rhinestone-studded bifocals attached with a dainty gold chain. The associate has a woman's classic and proper look from a decade past in her tailored dark suit and mid-length brunette bob.

"Do you have the receipt?" she asks.

"I do not."

"One moment, please," she says to Janet, holding up her pointer finger.

The sales associate turns and walks away to phone Ava from a small secure area behind the counter where a jeweler is seated at a low desk working no doubt on a glitzy piece of jewelry for some in-town celebrity or wealthy businessperson.

"Yes. Yes. Okay. Thank you, Ava."

Janet overhears this part of the conversation. When the sales associate reappears with a gloss-finished gift bag with twisted rope handles, Janet responds, "I understand about the phone call to Ava. Of course, you can't be too careful with these exquisite jewelry pieces."

The saleswoman looks again at Janet over the top of her bejeweled bifocals, now in a good-humored way, attempting to suppress a smile. "Be sure to show Ava the other items tucked inside the bag. The appraisal paper she requested and the design we've created for her matched earrings."

Janet leaves the store confused. *Was there something humorous I missed during this transaction?* she asks herself.

The parking valet brings Janet the Mercedes, and as she sets the gift bag beside her on the passenger seat, she admires the silvery bag's simple elegance, thinking how she might re-use it to carry a book around.

Then, just to be sure, she peeks inside the bag and removes the papers. *Yes, here is the appraisal paperwork for the necklace.*

"*Two hundred dollars?*" She says out loud in a disbelieving voice. "*Only two hundred dollars? I hope Ava didn't overpay for this necklace,*" she mumbles under her breath.

On the drive back to Ava's home, Janet imagines Cassandra Crawford as the *Cruella de Vil* of Diamond Lake. The pampered and arrogant Cassandra Crawford now with a choppy coif of spikey black and white hair and a penchant for taking puppies and turning them into fur coats. The overprivileged Cassandra Crawford. Her greed and vanity are so obvious to Janet. She wonders why Ava doesn't see it.

Ava's Friend? Hardly.

When Janet returns to the house, she's surprised to see Cassandra Crawford seated in a tight black dress and high heels, one arm casually draped over the back of Ava's orange corduroy sofa. Cassandra catches Janet's eye but looks away.

Guilty! Janet thinks to herself. *That's why she can't make eye contact with me. Guilty of adultery and taking advantage of Ava's vulnerability. Of course, these are just assumptions, she* reminds herself, with no *actual proof - yet.*

Janet hands the elegant jewelry store gift bag over to Ava. "Your appraisal paperwork and design sketch are tucked inside," she says in an understated manner.

Ava is putting on airs, playing the role of the leisure class elite. It pleases Ava immensely to be regarded with admiration, just as her late mother's fans were in adoring awe of her. *Always the daughter of Hollywood celebrities,* Janet thinks to herself.

Later, when Ava requests Janet's presence upstairs, the two are alone.

"What's this?" Ava asks from the comfort of her chair, holding the appraisal document at eye level.

"The appraisal document you requested for the amethyst necklace."

"How many zeros are there here?"

"Just two zeros, giving the necklace a value of two hundred dollars."

"Clearly, there's been a mistake!" Ava retorts with great indignance. She waves Janet out of the room, picking up the receiver to dial Cassandra Crawford.

Janet turns, intending to head back downstairs to her corner office but pauses on the landing when she overhears Ava's telephone conversation.

"Certainly, Cassandra. Yes. Yes. A mix-up. I understand. But can you understand *my* disappointment, knowing my longtime friend misrepresented the value of the necklace she sold to me? The jeweler's appraisal of this necklace is an embarrassment. Not sure I can set foot in that store again. How will they ever take me seriously? And what of the other jewelry? Perhaps I should appraise all of my jewelry from you to ensure there weren't other mix-ups?

Yes, yes. I'm listening.

No, no, I won't tell Nigel. Nigel is our family attorney, and we must maintain a positive professional relationship.

I understand. A one-time mistake, but if there were to be a scandal, our association with Nigel would undoubtedly taint the reputation of the Fleming Family Foundation as well.

Think of that, Cassandra, and of all the people you would bring down with you. My father often repeated this quote from Benjamin Franklin, 'It takes many good deeds to build a good reputation, and only one bad one to lose it.'

Please give this some careful thought, Cassandra.

I will place the amethyst necklace in a gift bag, and one of my girls will fetch it for you should you arrive when I am not at home."

Janet is astonished by her employer's coherent response. Ava's confidence and use of forceful words stop Janet in her tracks. *Was this Ava's alter ego talking? Where had this Ava been hiding all these months?*

Janet fist pumps an emphatic *"YES!"* and her expression changes to one of joyous satisfaction as she heads back downstairs to her lower-level office.

◆　◆　◆

"Can you believe it?" Janet says to Keegan over the phone from the comfort of her downtown apartment later that evening. "I told Ava of her mother's name change from Tasha Romanov to Beverly Rose Fleming and the story of her Russian grandfather and Palm Springs cousins almost three weeks ago, and she still hasn't mentioned it. Today, her focus was on a necklace sold to her by Cassandra Crawford. Cassandra conned Ava into buying an amethyst necklace of little value. Ava confronted Cassandra, which surprised me and warmed my heart a little, but priorities, priorities..."

"Maybe she just needs time to comprehend or appreciate the information you've discovered," Keegan responds in a calm voice.

"I must admit, Ava does seem more focused and thoughtful these days. More mindful of the day-to-day moments. I was truly amazed how she stood her ground with Cassandra this afternoon."

"Maybe the devotion you've shown Ava over these past few months has somehow empowered her," Keegan adds.

"Thank you. That's an encouraging thought."

Janet snuggles under a faux fur throw blanket on her sofa with a mug of hot chocolate in hand. Ava had been generous, letting her drive the Mercedes to and from work these early winter days. There were but a few snow flurries last week when Ava suggested that Janet drive the Mercedes home. 'It's safer,' she told Janet in two words.

Later that same evening, Richard asked Janet to move her car to a less conspicuous location. Her old Honda Accord was apparently an eyesore parked next to their luxury home.

A bit persnickety of him, she grumbled under her breath as she moved her vehicle to a far corner of the overflow parking area. *The old Honda Accord will soon be buried in snowdrifts anyway. One car indistinguishable from the next. So, why even bother?*

Janet redirects her thoughts and asks Keegan in a lighter voice, "Did you get a chance to make snow angels on your front lawn today?"

"You're my angel," Keegan says with a smile in his voice.

Janet sighs audibly. "In case you're wondering, that was a sigh of blissful contentment."

"Very reassuring," he responds. "Speaking of contentment, are you planning to spend the weekend? I have a great dinner planned for us."

"Something we can make together, I hope. It's always more fun cooking *with you*! Just wondering," Janet says, switching to a more serious tone of voice, "speaking hypothetically, of course, do you believe Ava's ancestral ghosts have found an iota of peace since our Palm Springs visit?"

"Well, we certainly did what we could to connect those past and present. Hopefully, everyone here and in the afterlife has benefitted."

"How many spirits do you think there are?" Janet

asks.

"You would know better than me. How many spiritual ancestors do *you* think there are?"

"Ava's parents: Beverly Rose and Sebastian. That's two. Pretty sure I saw them my first night house-sitting. Most likely, Beverly Rose left the necklace *'Forever'* behind that night. The next morning, I found it on the floor outside Ava's jewelry-safe room."

Janet sips her hot chocolate contemplating the inexplicable mysteries of the past few months.

"There is an emotional connection to that necklace," she adds. "Ava wore it, and her mother, Beverly Rose wore it for the movie *Forever,* and then Sebastian's mistress wore a copy of the necklace. Maybe in the spirit world, Beverly Rose has forgiven her husband, Sebastian, for his dalliances. That's Hollywood, or at least it was in those days. Think Spencer Tracy and Katherine Hepburn. Famous couple. Spencer Tracy was married, but not to Katherine Hepburn."

"Then there's Duchess Zara and her Russian fiancé Mishka Vasiliev," Keegan says, "that makes four."

"Do you think Ava's California cousins will ever contact her? They are now part of this family's narrative. Will there ever be a family reunion of sorts?" Janet asks.

"Kahil Gibran says, '*Life unfolds itself in mysterious ways.*' Be patient." Keegan advises.

"You read poetry as well? You amaze me! I'll bring wine and dessert, and we can read our favorite poems to each other by candlelight."

Janet closes her eyes and tips her head back onto the pillowed sofa. She snuggles under her warm blanket, grateful for Keegan's imagination and sensitivity.

◆ ◆ ◆

Saturday morning at Keegan's...

Janet picks up Keegan's coffee table issue of *Lake Winds North magazine*. The magazine falls open in her hands to a colorful section of prominent people attending social and fund-raising events about town.

She flips through the magazine, wondering if she might recognize one of Ava's long-standing acquaintances among the glossy photos. To her immediate surprise, there is a three-quarter page photo of Ava decked out in a splash of gold and diamond jewelry, smiling a gorgeous, radiant movie star smile. Janet has never seen Ava smile so radiantly, so beautifully. Come to think of it, Janet rarely sees Ava smile. But there she is, smiling like Hollywood's darling of darlings. The 'orphaned royal'.

And there is Cassandra Crawford, head tilted coyly, standing shoulder to shoulder beside her longtime quasi-celebrity friend, Ava Fleming, using her wily tricks to attract the attention of photographers and presenting herself as one of the grand dames of local society. One hand fanned dramatically across her chest as if caught in a moment of breathless delight. Her slightly spooky, pointy extensions of fingernails, a shade of deep burgundy nail polish to match her cunning, gothic application of burgundy lipstick, and excessive use of mascara and eye shadow. Her enhanced looks drawing the attention of onlookers.

And there, adding insult to injury, in a far corner of the photo, is Maxwell. His body captured in a blur of motion, but with his head turned, Janet can clearly see him leering at Cassandra.

Janet grimaces. "How did I miss this lavish event?" she asks, holding the picture up for Keegan to see as he prepares breakfast. "Usually, I'm the one fact-gathering and making arrangements for Ava to attend one of these ridiculously posh parties."

"My Uncle Gerald and Sheila threw a party when we were away in Palm Springs those two weeks—a rather spur-of-the-moment affair, celebrating an old friend's birthday. Sheila told me Ava arrived in a limo with Cassandra and Maxwell. They arrived and left together."

Keegan stirs egg and milk in a mixing bowl, then holds a bottle of maple syrup high enough for Janet to see, and she nods, 'Yes.'

"Sorry. Didn't mean to sound disrespectful toward your Uncle Gerald, but how could Ava...." Janet stops herself midsentence.

"How could Ava, what?" Keegan asks as he melts butter into a cast iron skillet.

"How could Ava dismiss the antics of these so-called friends that con her and selfishly use her? Either she is very forgiving, or she accepts them for who they are, character flaws and all. Maybe she doesn't care about the money. She has enough of it."

Janet watches Keegan drop thick slices of bread soaked in a mixture of eggs with milk and cinnamon into the frying pan. The delicious aroma of sizzling cinnamon on toast promises an indulgent breakfast served hot with butter and maple syrup.

"Maybe it's more important for Ava to be part of the community that sets itself apart as the upper-class gentry of Diamond Lake," Keegan suggests.

"Maybe so..." Janet responds as she looks down at the magazine still in her hands.

"Oh, did I mention Maxwell has the lakeside property he inherited from Beverly Rose up for sale?

Would you grab us a couple of plates from the cupboard behind me, my sweetness?"

"*What?!* Oh, yes," Janet answers, now feeling somewhat befuddled as she sets the magazine down on the kitchen counter.

She walks to the cupboard, reaches for two plates, selects silverware from the lower drawer behind Keegan, and sets them on the counter beside him. Then leaning in with breathless anticipation, "Tell me more about Maxwell's property," she says.

"My Uncle Gerald plans to buy the property from Maxwell and turn it into a recreational facility. He would like to put a boat house on the property for the Diamond Lake Yacht Club. He asked if I would take charge or assist as General Manager. Gather the youth and teens who would like to learn to sail. Maybe offer classes, instruction...."

With a quickened heartbeat and a look of yearning, Janet asks, "Can I help?"

"You know how to sail?" Keegan asks.

"No, but I could help you organize the groups, and you could teach me along with everyone else!"

"So, you want to be my protégé?" Keegan asks with a wink.

"Of course I do!' Janet answers with an air of readiness, clasping her hands prayerfully.

CHAPTER EIGHTEEN

THE PROMISE OF FOREVER

Today, like most mornings, Janet and Keegan have laced up their hiking boots, grabbed a set of trekking poles, and hit the trails to experience the natural splendor and wonder of the forested area surrounding their lakeside home.

The rhythm of the trek puts them in a quiet, meditative mood. Janet senses this day's all-embracing spiritual warmth as birds call to each other from treetops of color and light and squirrels rustle in an overhang of branches, then scurry down the tree trunk one behind the other.

Trees of fiery red, shimmery gold, and vibrant orange fragrance the air with the earthy scent of autumn and reminder of another passing season.

Janet's mind drifts as she imagines a post-hike appetizer of fresh bruschetta and how their exceptionally sweet garden-grown tomatoes will taste combined with olive oil, basil, and mozzarella on garlic toast when they take an unexpected turn down Ladyslipper Lane.

"Oh!" Janet says to Keegan, stopping suddenly and looking up at the jagged wooden street sign, "Let's check on Ava's estate! Elaine told me Ava's home has been sitting vacant for a while. Let's just peek in the windows."

Keegan nods in agreement.

They approach Ava's home with an air of hesitant curiosity. *Might they be trespassing?*

Janet approaches the elongated entry door window to peek inside the house, then notices the front entrance door is slightly ajar. She taps on the weighty door with one of her trekking poles, and to her surprise, it groans open on stiff brass hinges. Janet and Keegan step quietly inside.

They peer through an atmosphere of dust suspended in streams of chalky light to see a haphazard arrangement of furniture draped - as though floated into position - in sheets of white. The room is hushed with illusion. The vague outline of sheets, whispers of time fading in, fading out.

Janet winces, then sneezes, shifting her position in the front foyer as a gust of fresh lake air breezes in through the open door.

Twenty years have passed since Janet first entered this home to fill the position of Personal Assistant to the owner of the estate, Ava Fleming. The job opportunity with Ava led her to meet Keegan Scott, now her devoted partner, and together, they oversee the popular recreation area on Diamond Lake owned by Keegan's uncle Gerald Scott. *Life is good.* She has much to be thankful for.

Janet's eyes prickle with tears. Lost in a state of reverie and fond memories, she pauses to examine the space around her. Yes, this is familiar. The console table on her right. This is where it sat. Yet, curiously, it is bare, undraped. She touches the cool surface lightly with her fingertips, remembering. White stone on iron legs, centered below the vintage French wall mirror adorned with filigree bursts of gold metal roses.

Her pale head and upper body are reflected in the glass like the unsettling image of someone who has blurred past. *Her past...*

Janet watches as, wide-eyed and ready to explore, Keegan wanders down the hall, around the corner, and out of sight.

She turns back to focus on the great room before her, remembering the oversized splashes of avant-garde wall art. The clean white lines of sleek leather couches and chairs in the formal lounging and dining areas, the assortment of tables constructed of iron, stone, ornamental golds, and even the two circular side-by-side Tiffany crystal dining tables resting on milky white floating swan pedestals.

It would take two handymen and a shout-out to the gardener to rearrange the furniture on any given day that the lady of the house felt dissatisfied with some aspect of daily life.

Janet recalls the drop-ins, the self-absorbed socialites that paused here, perhaps straight from the country club, to play 'mirror-mirror-on-the-wall' before entering the elongated rooms in the luxurious home of Ava Fleming. They were the 'lake people', dwelling in multi-generational homes that were monuments of historical architecture, featuring bay windows holding spectacular views of blue sky and drifting waves. She recalls their blasé reaction to

Ava Fleming's upscale furnishings, to her wall of windows, framing million-dollar views of Diamond Lake. Once, their vanities and eccentricities puzzled her, and she would observe them with a pragmatic sideways glance. But now, she understands their motivations were for personal attention and social recognition.

Stepping forward, silken spider webs entangle Janet in a fragile breath of fright. She takes a half-step back, brushing cobwebs from her hair and face. She looks down the hallway, searching for Keegan. He is still out of sight when she hears the faintest murmur of voices, reminding her of the housekeepers chatting on a coffee break from the kitchen at the far end of the home. But this was not possible. There are no housekeepers or bookkeepers in employment. *The house is unoccupied.*

Janet quietly gazes past the draped furniture and out the windows, recalling the somber occasion of Ava's funeral and Richard's mournful expression.

The lady of the house now lay at rest just beyond the stately swing of cemetery gates beneath the outstretched arms of the angel, Gabriel. A bronze monument on a square granite base with large vertical wings, standing in the very presence of God. The angel's watchful gaze falls over a family of verdant cemetery plots, including Ava's celebrity mother and father – once Hollywood royalty - Ava, and the plot beside Ava, where her husband Richard would eventually be laid to rest.

Keegan reappears with an unfocused gaze. Still looking around. So much to take in. *Remember.*

Then, at once, in unison, they glance toward the wall of lakeside windows. Janet and Keegan are startled to see what appears to be the groundskeeper. *Had he been standing there all along?*

Janet feels lightheaded, uncertain of her response to what appears before her. Meanwhile, Keegan is openly staring at the vaguely familiar man.

"Sorry to intrude," Janet says apologetically and somewhat embarrassed. "I once worked for the owner of this home. I was the personal assistant to Ava Fleming. Just wondering what became of her estate. That's all."

The groundskeeper smiles wistfully but says nothing as he draws back. The sunlight seems to be absorbing him. It's difficult to see the entire outline of his body or facial features with the light pouring over him, *or is it through him?*

"We were just planning to peek in the windows, but the front door was open, so we let ourselves in," Janet explains.

"Kind of sad that this remarkable home has been abandoned," Keegan adds, staring hard at the ambiguous figure of a man standing across the room from them, bathed in an aura of gauzy light.

"Not abandoned," the groundskeeper responds in a voice resonant with a deep European accent. "Ava's Palm Springs, California cousins were quite happy with their inheritance and will be moving into Ava's home next season. And most prominently displayed here," he says, bowing while extending his arm in a grand gesture of introduction, "will be the oil portrait of Duchess Zara, and beside Duchess Zara will be a portrait the family has commissioned of Zara's fiancé Mishka Vasiliev."

Although it is unclear exactly where the groundskeeper is indicating the portraits be hung, Janet wants to keep the man talking in hopes of gleaning more information.

"So, Ava's entire estate has been inherited by her California cousins, who are moving here? To Diamond Lake, into Ava's home?" she asks.

"Yes," the groundskeeper answers, "It is to link the ancestors. It is peace for the souls that cannot exist one without the other. This home will be a place for love and the memory of love to flow through."

"Such poetic words," Janet says, getting goosebumps. "Almost prayerful. Thank you for allowing me, or us rather," she says, nodding to Keegan, "to relive this memory of our beloved, late Ava Fleming."

As they turn toward the front entry door, the room glimmers with wavelike motions of light. The air suddenly heavy with the weight and importance of an other-worldly presence.

Janet feels an immediate twinge of recognition and pauses. Then, digging into her shoulder-slung fanny pack for her cell phone asks, "Would you mind if I take one last picture of Ava's home before we leave, as a keepsake?"

But when Keegan and Janet turn back, the groundskeeper is gone! Vanished, it seems, into thin air. Reminding Janet of her first day at Ava Fleming's home when she sent a lofty wish into the air on a seeded fluff of white cotton and watched it disappear into the wild blue imagination of afternoon sky. On that day, she had asked God for an interesting story. *That, indeed, it has been.*

In the next moment, white sheets covering the furniture lift and billow spontaneously in a pearly shimmer of iridescence, awakened by the faintest sight of spirits passing through the room.

It is in this prolonged moment of passing that the spirits pause, just long enough for Janet and Keegan to hear a whisper of words echo around them,

"Believing doesn't depend on knowing, only trusting that there's more. There's always more,"

...as the mystical nature of time moves forward into the late afternoon light with the promise of forever.

ACKNOWLEDGMENTS

I wrote ***Thirteen Diamond Lake Point – A Spirited Mystery*** under the spell of the local folk of Diamond Lake (a fictional town in a well-to-do suburb of Minneapolis) and the whimsical upper-class gentry, glaring character flaws and all.

Writing this story was a bittersweet journey along life's lakeside path, complete with romance, daydreams, and disappointment.

I thank the real-life characters whose eccentricities and fantastic life stories fueled my imagination. To those who have passed from this earth, you are forever in my heart. Thank you for allowing me to channel you.

Everlasting gratitude (from this life and beyond) to my late husband, John, my parents, Janet Crawford and Fredrick Crawford, and lifelong friends Mary Topel and Thomas C. Shooltz for your ongoing encouragement and support.

To my dear writer friends –

Phyllis Dozier, Laura Jensen, David Landskroener, Nadia Giordana, and Deb Moore

…you arrived just in time with your wordsmith super-powers and dazzling air of playfulness and mysticism. You offered keen insights and kept my creative energy flowing. I love you all.

Thanks also to my publisher, Ann Aubitz of Fuzion-Press, for her fresh, intuitive responses during the creation of this book.

And really, how could I not acknowledge my first boyfriend, Jim Murphy, whose reaction to my incessant questioning never missed a beat with his usual response:

"What are you, writing a book?"

I may now answer, *"Yes. It just took me four and a half decades to get there."*

www.ingramcontent.com/pod-product-compliance
Lightning Source LLC
Chambersburg PA
CBHW071145260626
47162CB00003B/929